UNTWINE

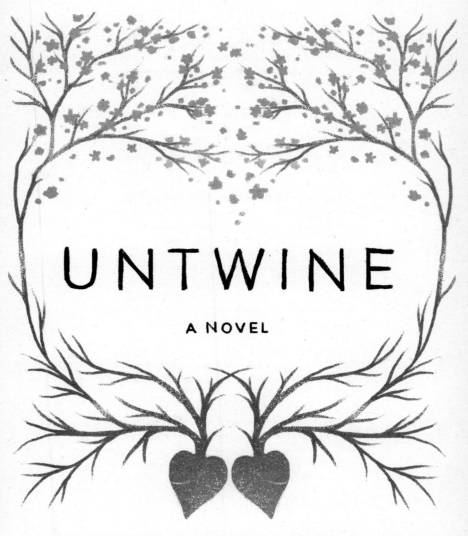

UNTWINE

A NOVEL

EDWIDGE DANTICAT

Scholastic Inc.

This book was originally published in hardcover by Scholastic Press in 2015.

The publisher does not have any control over and does not assume any responsibility for author or third-party websites or their content.

This book is a work of fiction. Names, characters, places, and incidents are either the product of the author's imagination or are used fictitiously, and any resemblance to actual persons, living or dead, business establishments, events, or locales is entirely coincidental.

ISBN 978-0-545-42304-5

10 9 8 7 6 5 4 3   17 18 19 20 21

Printed in the U.S.A.   40
First printing 2017

Book design by Elizabeth B. Parisi

For Manman

You are my sister . . .
You are my face; you are me . . .
I waited for you
You are mine
You are mine
You are mine

—TONI MORRISON
Beloved

UNTWINE

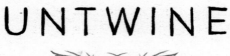

I REMEMBER WHAT was playing when the car slammed into us. It was Igor Stravinsky's *The Firebird*. Like most pieces of classical music I've ever heard, it started out pretty slow, then sped up, then peaked, then slowed down again. My sister, Isabelle, asked Dad to put her orchestra practice CD in his SUV's new, super-fancy, twelve-disk player. Isabelle unbuckled her seat belt, leaned over, and handed the CD to Dad from the backseat. Isabelle wanted to hear the music as the "Maestro" had intended it, she said, before she and her friends butchered it at Morrison High's spring orchestra concert.

The car ride was a quiet one because our parents had announced two weeks earlier that they were separating. They had even stopped wearing their wedding rings. We were all still living under the same roof, until Dad could find a place of his own and move out.

"You want us to wait for you, or do you want to get a bite with your friends?" Mom lowered the volume on *The Firebird* to ask Isabelle.

"If we'd left fifteen minutes earlier, we would have missed all this traffic." Dad sounded irritated.

Even though he had sworn that nothing was going to change, that he would still "accompany" Mom to our school activities whenever he could, I was thinking that the four of us wouldn't be eating together that much from now on, so I hoped Isabelle would choose us over her friends, at least for the night.

"Can Ron come with?" Isabelle asked.

Ron Johnson was a relatively new friend. I didn't know much about him, except that he didn't run around with Isabelle's music crowd. He liked pilot whales, bird-watching, rock climbing, and all types of other outdoorsy things. He was a nature geek, like Isabelle.

"Sure he can come," Dad said. He had calmed down a bit and was adjusting his muscular build in the driver's seat. His voice was cool, but his hands weren't. He was looking over the long line of cars ahead of us. They were packed so closely together that their lights seemed to merge. There was nowhere for him to go.

At first it seemed like a mirage, some type of optical illusion, like when water distorts light and the light gets misdirected. Suddenly the traffic began moving forward, then a red minivan sped up, crossed the middle lane, and slammed into the back door, on Isabelle's side.

I remember Isabelle trying to face me, her long thin braids, which were the same length as mine—our only concession to twindom—grazing her shoulders, then covering her face like a shield. She raised both her hands to her eyes at the same moment that Mom started screaming.

"*Vire!* Turn! *Vire!*" Mom shouted in the mix of English and Haitian Creole that she and Dad sometimes spoke, especially when they were anxious or angry.

But even as the cars around us tried to scurry out of the way and Dad did his best to follow their lead, there was still nowhere to turn. On one side of us was a concrete wall protecting a gated community from the street. Dad tried to steer the car as close to the wall as possible and as Mom's and my doors dragged against the wall, the tension created fireworks-like sparks. The scraping was loud, too, like thousands of fingernails against as many blackboards. I remember thinking that even if we made it out of this okay, between all the screeching and Mom's screaming, and the other cars on the street honking, we'd all be deaf for a long time.

The red minivan rammed into Isabelle's door one more time.

"Turn the other way. *Lòt kote a!*" Mom yelled, then began coughing as the smell of burning tires filled the inside of the car.

And here I am prolonging this so I can spend a little more time in this part of my life, in Dad's SUV, on an ordinary Friday evening heading to a concert where my sister was supposed to play.

In this part of my life, my sister, Isabelle, and I are identical twins, as identical as two drops of water, my grandparents liked to say, even though it's not completely true. Yes, we are both tall, five feet and eleven inches, like our dad. But Isabelle and I each have a small dot of a birthmark, on opposite sides, behind our ears. We are different in other ways, too. Even though I like to draw and think of myself as an artist—a future one anyway—I'd rather swim a hundred laps at high noon in the Miami sun than play the flute or the piano.

Before the second, bigger crash, I remember Isabelle saying, "The flute. The flute."

At first I thought it was because she was worried about the flute, but as Dad's car swerved closer and closer to the wall, the black leather flute case shot up from Isabelle's lap to her face, then bounced off her chin, pushing her head into the side window. The side window cracked, and I like to think that it was the impact of the red minivan, and not Isabelle's head, that shattered the glass. Still, the flute case bounced back and struck the other side of Isabelle's face, before pounding into her ribs.

People say that things like this happen in slow motion, as though you suddenly become an astronaut in the antigravity chamber of your own life. This wasn't true for me. Things were speeding up instead, and I did my best to slow them down in my mind.

Mom was still screaming our names, taking turns calling Isabelle and me by both our proper names and our nicknames: Isabelle, Giselle, Iz, Giz, Izzie, Gizzie. She then called Dad ("David! David! David!"), shouting his name over and over again.

Isabelle didn't need to call my name. Not because of the twin telepathy thing people always talk about, but because we were holding hands. We were holding hands the tightest we have ever held hands in our entire lives. We were holding hands just as we had been holding hands on the day we were born. We had shared the same amniotic sac, and during Mom's C-section, the doctor told our parents that he would need to untwine our fingers to separate us. We were born holding hands. And now, even as our heads bobbed and our bodies flopped— mine strapped behind the seat belt and Isabelle's loose and unprotected—we screamed for our parents, who were screaming for us, but we wouldn't let go.

Our parents, too, were being thrown around up front behind their seat belts. The backs of their heads emerged, then disappeared, their faces striking the air bags, Mom's petite, reed-thin body and Dad's muscular one trying to stay upright.

Then it happened. The ultimate crash. The light that we couldn't escape hammered into us, mashing in Isabelle's air bag–less door.

My sister was still holding my hand, but now our hands were wet and sticky, and hot. I heard Isabelle moan, then gasp, as though exasperated. "We're going to be late," she said, while gasping for breath.

We're late, we're late, for a very important date, I thought, as though we had fallen deep down into a series of rabbit holes. *No time to say hello, goodbye, we're late.*

I don't know if Isabelle actually said anything about us being late. Maybe she was just thinking it. Maybe I was just thinking it.

Then there was an eerie silence, pierced by sirens, then honks and beeps, like birds chirping, but unfamiliar birds, or just one, a golden firebird, glowing at a distance, tempting you to touch it, knowing you never could.

In the version of the Russian folktale my sister loves—the one that inspired the centerpiece of the school orchestra's spring concert that night—a king orders his three sons to capture the shimmering firebird that had been stealing the king's golden apples. But when the youngest son tries to capture the bird, all he ends up with is a single feather. Though bright enough to light several rooms, the feather isn't good enough for the king, who would settle for nothing but the bird itself. The king's youngest son then goes on a quest that leads not only to him capturing the firebird, but meeting a protective grey wolf and a beautiful princess. On his way to the happy ending, the prince gets killed by his brothers. The grey wolf then brings the prince back to life with a secret potion called the Water of Life, and the happy ending is restored.

I wish it could be the same for my parents and my sister.

I wish it could be the same for me.

The secret potion.

The water of life.

All of it.

When I wake up, I am in an ambulance. My whole body feels heavy, but not in pain. I don't know if I've been given pain-killers or if I'm just in shock.

I have an oxygen mask on my face and a brace around my neck. I can't speak to the faces floating in and out of my view, as a piercing light is beamed into my eyes. I can hear static over a radio and try to capture a word here and there. They mostly talk in letters and shorthand. I remember ETA (Estimated Time of Arrival) and BP (Blood Pressure). Because one is thought to be too long and the other too low.

I wonder where my parents are. Are they also in ambulances, with their own acronyms being shouted over their heads?

There are moments during the ambulance ride—which I am prolonging here, too—moments when I'm not even there, when I can't hear the sirens or feel the hard board beneath my body. These are brief moments of silence, like they demand at assemblies, or after something horrible has happened.

Should I be praying? I ask myself.

Our parents have always been religious, but Isabelle and I have often stood, as Isabelle likes to say, on the margins between belief and disbelief. Our faith is a mishmash of many things. We believe in family, in music and art, but we mostly believe in each other. We love our minister, though, Pastor Ben. He was the one who christened us. We also like the church youth choir. Isabelle plays the flute for them and I sing alto with my best friend, Tina. We like the church building's high, gabled ceilings. We like the dark burgundy cushioned pews. We love Mom's cloche hats and Dad's Sunday morning black and navy suits. We love how we all sit together in our favorite mid-row pew. Will we still sit together after our parents separate?

Whatever is after this world, I pray that there's room for the four of us to always sit together. In the afterworld, let there be music for Isabelle and drawing pencils and pads for me. Let there be fellow army vet pals for Dad and clients for him to defend—even though I don't think there'll be people needing political asylum in heaven. Let there be yoga classes for Mom and news anchors' faces for her to transform with makeup. Let there be Haitian food, rice and beans and fried pork, *griyo*, and pumpkin soup, especially on January 1, when we celebrate Haitian Independence Day by drinking bowl after bowl.

If there is a heaven, it should be like all the places you love or the places you've never been but wish you'd visited while you were still alive. For Isabelle, that would be some of the music capitals of the world but mostly New Orleans, where she would listen to live jazz, twenty-four hours a day.

For me, heaven would be the Louvre, where I would see the *Mona Lisa* in person. It would also be Haiti, where Mom and Dad were born and fell in love and where Isabelle and I sometimes spend summers with Dad's parents, Grandma Régine and Grandpa Marcus. Grandma Régine and Grandpa Marcus promised to have a big party for Isabelle and me at their house, at the beginning of this coming summer, for our seventeenth birthday.

These are the things I want to shout inside the ambulance. These are the things I don't want to forget. I want to hold on to this ambulance ride for as long as I can, because maybe that's all I have left.

CHAPTER 2

WE'RE LATE, WE'RE late, for a very important date. No time to say hello, goodbye, we're late, we're late.

My eyes ache when they pull me out of the ambulance. Dozens of new faces are staring down at me, countless hands transferring me from the flat board to a gurney. Voices drown out one another as my jeans and gold-sequined blouse are clipped off with scissors. My skin feels way too hot, like it's melting, falling away.

More injuries are listed than I have operating body parts:

Depressed skull fracture

Cerebral and lung contusions

Liver laceration

Intracranial pressure and edema

Unstable pelvic fracture

And on and on . . .

That's when I realize they're not just talking about me, but about both of us. They're also talking about Isabelle.

In a situation like mine, a lot of people say that they see a bright light, then levitate towards it, away from their bodies. Then their lives flash before their eyes, until they meet a comforting angel, their own firebird, or grey wolf, or beautiful princess, or dead relative who encourages them to float back into their skin and remain among the living. The bright light I see is my sister. She is still sitting next to me in our father's SUV. And because she doesn't have her phone with her (why doesn't she have her phone with her?), she's listening to the music the old-school way, on a CD, the music that she and her friends are about to play. She's looking out the window, day-dreaming perhaps about a flawless performance or a kiss from chocolate-skinned Ron Johnson. Though the kiss might have been hard to manage with all of us there. Or maybe she's think-ing about our parents' separation, how we might not be together, all four of us, as a family anymore. Or maybe she's worried that some strangers might soon invade our little unit, in a few weeks, months: our parents' future girlfriends and boyfriends, the stepsiblings we'd never allow ourselves to love.

With our parents' coming separation, our little fortress was crumbling, and sitting in that car, we all knew it. But there's something about music, when you feel it deeply, when you understand it so well, the way Isabelle understands it, there is something about it that makes scary things seem to disappear. If only for a little while.

Even while looking out the window, Isabelle might not have seen the car coming at us. Before that, I'd been looking out the window, too, but I was only seeing things on my side of the car, things that were different from what she was seeing. I wasn't examining any greater truths. I was looking at headlights and fidgeting drivers. I saw a lady turn around and yell at three young boys crammed in the back of her compact hybrid car. The boys were wearing soccer uniforms. They looked like they were the same age, but they were black and white and brown. The brown woman, maybe not the mother of all of them, looked tired. The boys kept passing a soccer ball back and forth behind her, and this seemed to be making her even more tired each time she took her eyes off the traffic and turned around and told them to stop.

I saw a man inhale a whole hamburger, then wash it down with sixteen ounces of Coke. I saw an older woman smoke three cigarettes in a row. I wanted to point these things out to Isabelle and my parents as they sat in the stalled traffic with me, lost in their own thoughts. But after a while the music gave us all a way out of speaking to each other. Silence was always our best form of agreement.

In being silent, we were also being considerate of Isabelle.

She was in "preparation mode" as Mom and Dad liked to say, and usually I would have made a joke about her little high school orchestra not being the New York Philharmonic and us not being on our way to Carnegie Hall, but this time I said nothing. After all, we were late. Late to an important date.

I can only get myself so far back in my memory and even then with so many gaps in between. It is as if my memory has become the inside of our father's car, Stravinsky, the flute box, the red light shattering through glass, and the voice that says over and over again, urgently at first, then in a lulling whisper, "I think we're going to be late."

Later, I'm thinking I'm still inside Dad's car, still moving. But I am alone in a small white room with a large glass window panel overlooking a brightly lit hallway, where people walk by with their heads bowed.

I actually feel pain now, too much to pinpoint, too massive, too everywhere. But worse than the pain is my mind's racing, like the feet of the people rushing back and forth, as if towards or away from some greater danger elsewhere.

Outside my room, the occasional doctor and nurse dash towards beeps and screams and "codes." And already I have a new vocabulary. How do I even know that a code's bells and whistles and alarms mean that someone might be dying? Maybe it's because I heard it being shouted a bunch of times in the ambulance. Had it been shouted at Isabelle? Did we both code at some point? Did Mom and Dad code?

That mind speak, that connection people think only twins have, can also apply to other people who love each other deeply. Soon after our parents announced they were separating, Isabelle and I could still hear Mom's sobs a few minutes after watching her drive away from the house, on her way to a yoga class.

I hope I can ask questions when someone finally comes to pay attention to me in this little white room. The silver lining might be that I must not be so bad if I am being left alone. The worse you are, the more people crowd around you, right?

I am in the PICU. I can see the words PEDIATRIC INTENSIVE CARE UNIT printed in bold black letters on the glass panel window that takes up half the wall. I'm reading backwards. Or is it upside down? Or am I reading at all?

I think I'm being watched through that glass window. Or on a monitor. Sometimes it's easy to feel when people are watching you. Maybe somewhere a nurse or a doctor is sitting behind a desk, watching a bunch of people like me. That same person could be watching over Isabelle, too.

I can barely keep track of all the random and not so random thoughts drifting in and out of my head. Maybe that's a good sign. Then I remember our cat, Dessalines, who I imagine pacing between our front door and the litter box, scratching the wooden floors, wondering where we are. I wonder how long it will take someone to find Dessalines, if none of us goes home. He might have to wait a while before Josiane, our cleaning lady, stops by, as she does once a week.

Dessalines will have to live up to his namesake now. He'll have to prove himself worthy of the Haitian revolutionary hero Dad named him after. Like us, he'll have to fight for his survival.

It was Dad's idea to name our copper-eyed black Burmese Dessalines. Dad takes every opportunity he can to teach us lessons about Haitian history, even making a hero into a cat, a cat into a hero. It's a good way to teach someone a lesson, though. You have to learn about the real Dessalines if you're walking down the street and looking for your cat—as Isabelle and I often find ourselves doing—and your confused friends ask why your cat's name is not something like *Kitty*.

Mom's older sister, Aunt Leslie, lives in Orlando, but she will definitely come down as soon as she hears what happened. She's a pediatrician, not a veterinarian, but she would save Dessalines. Or maybe Dad's younger brother, Uncle Patrick, will come down from New York to save Dessalines.

Aunt Leslie arrives late for Thanksgiving dinner every year. There is always one last patient to see. Her patients, she often says, are the children she'll never have.

"You twins." She always refers to us together as *you twins*. "You twins are getting older by the minute. My patients are getting born by the minute. They keep coming and coming."

And now we might be going and going, slipping away. And her own sister might be slipping away, too, somewhere. And what if we all slipped away, how would she answer now when she was asked if she had children?

"No," she might say, "but I used to have twin nieces who were just like my own children."

And how would our parents answer—if they're alive—when people asked if they had children? Would they say, "Two," the way they have in the past, then add, "twin girls. I mean, young ladies."

We were the first twins on both sides of our families. We were always *les filles*, "the girls," or *les jumelles*, to our grand-parents. Mom said that she and Dad chose the names they did for us so that they could rhyme a little bit with *jumelle*, the word for "female twin" in French. Our middle names are the first names of each of our grandmothers, so I am Giselle Sandrine Boyer, for my grandma on Mom's side, and my sister is Isabelle Régine Boyer, for Dad's mom.

In Haitian Creole, the word for "twin" is *marasa*. If we had a sibling follow us, a brother or a sister, that child would have been our *dosa*, the "untwinned" one. When we were little, Isabelle and I promised our parents that if we had a brother or sister, we would never make him or her feel left out. We would teach the *dosa* our twin speak, we told our parents, what Isabelle called "the language of the palms," because sometimes when we had something urgent to say to each other, we would just grab each other's hands, or gesture.

Aunt Leslie is our godmother. When we get mad at our mother, we call Aunt Leslie our "good" mother, because if our parents refused to get something for us, we'd call her up and she would send it. Dolls. Clothes. And later, money. We'd send her links to things online, and she'd buy them and have them mailed to us directly. I wish I could call her now to tell her to go save Dessalines.

"Go save Dessalines?" She'd try to make a joke out of it. "Well, he's been dead for over two hundred years," she'd say. And she would force me to say it even though she knew exactly what I meant. "Dessalines the cat, Aunt Leslie, not the revolutionary. We need you to save Dessalines the cat."

Surely the hospital would call Aunt Leslie and Uncle Patrick, or even Grandma Régine and Grandpa Marcus in Haiti, and they would go by the house and find Dessalines.

In the middle of all this imagining of Dessalines's rescue, all of a sudden, I open my eyes and see Aunt Leslie sitting there in the only chair at my bedside. She is holding my hand the way Isabelle was holding my hand in the car.

For once Aunt Leslie is the first one to arrive, and she is never the first one to arrive. Aunt Leslie is even wearing her white doctor's coat over her black blouse and slacks, as though she hasn't had a second to pull the coat off. Or maybe it's because just as she's always told us, they treat you better in hospitals when you have a doctor in the family. Maybe she's purposely kept it on. Or maybe they have given her privileges. This was part of her vocabulary. She'd told us all about "privileges," permission to use a hospital's facilities as a doctor. But they certainly wouldn't have given her privileges to work on us. She must have simply forgotten to take off her coat before getting in her car, or on the plane.

I remember Aunt Leslie telling Isabelle and me at our weekend-long twelfth birthday party—hosted by Aunt Leslie and attended by our family and Tina's family at Disney World—that in some places people thought twins were bad omens. When they were born, their parents left them out in the forest to die. In other places twins were revered and even worshipped. In some parts of Haiti, for example, twins were thought to have special powers, and if you didn't give them what they wanted, they could put spells on you. Maybe that's what Isabelle and I had done to her. Maybe our love had put a spell on her. We loved her so much that we made her love us even more. Maybe that's what brought her to my bedside so quickly.

At the Disney World birthday party weekend, after scaring us with her twin stories, Aunt Leslie gave each of us an identical gold chain with a hand-shaped pendant with what seemed like vines carved inside. They were good luck charms, she'd said, from the Maghreb region of Northwest Africa. She had bought them for us while attending a medical conference in Cairo. They were called the Hand of Fatima and were meant to protect us from the evil eye.

"Why do we need protection from the evil eye if we have special powers?" I asked her.

"Just put it on," my sister had shouted.

Where's my necklace now, I wonder. Neither Isabelle nor I had taken them off since Aunt Leslie had given them to us. How come I am only thinking of it now?

At times it feels like my ears are filled with water. Sometimes they feel crystal clear, almost too clear, so that the machines in my room and other rooms and their stop-and-go beeping feel like missile attacks directed at my brain. Sometimes it feels much too bright in the room, even though the lights are dimmed. Sometimes it feels too dark, like I am going blind.

Standing behind Aunt Leslie's chair is a policewoman dressed all in black. She has a shiny star on her chest and a pad and pencil in her hands. The light coming off her star is blinding.

The policewoman looks tall, even to someone as tall as me. So tall that she seems like a giant standing next to Aunt Leslie.

"I want to see if I can question her," the policewoman says. "Even with hand signals."

"It's only been a few hours," Aunt Leslie says, "and she has a very bad concussion."

"According to the ER doctor, she might be floating in and out of consciousness," the policewoman says. "The sooner we get a statement from her, the better."

"She's in no condition. As you can see," Aunt Leslie says, reminding me of the tube that I want to reach over and grab out of my mouth, except that my hands are tied down, as if I am a prisoner and not a patient. There are spaces between my teeth. I've possibly lost teeth, whole teeth, pieces of teeth. With the tube pressing my tongue down, there's not enough room for my tongue to find out exactly how many, but I have more stubs than teeth, fragments, pieces, shards of teeth.

"She's in no condition," Aunt Leslie repeats to herself.

Tears are streaming down her face. I have never seen Aunt Leslie cry before, not even at her own mother, Grandma Sandrine's, funeral. Now she's sobbing so much that the officer has to reach down and squeeze her shaking shoulder. I wonder if Aunt Leslie knows where Mom and Dad are. I wonder if she knows where Isabelle is.

Aunt Leslie puts both her hands on top of mine. Aunt Leslie's hands feel soft, and even though they're sweaty and shaky, they feel like being home with Mom, Dad, Isabelle, and Dessalines. They feel like love.

"I'm sorry," the officer says. "But we think what happened was not exactly an accident. We're just trying to figure things out."

What happened was not exactly an accident.

I hear those words, then sink under.

Down, down, down. Would the fall never *come to an end! "I wonder how many miles I've fallen . . . I wonder if I shall fall right* through *the earth!"*

Under is now a dark empty space that I slip into when my mind wants to rest. When things become too difficult to process, I sink under. And while I am under, I remember some things and not others. Under can be a blank space, like an empty sketch pad or canvas, or an empty room. Or a classroom.

This year in the art history class that Isabelle refused to take, we learned about rock engravings and cave paintings. I doubt that with my unmoving hands I could even carve a single letter on a cave wall now.

I have become prehistoric, I want to tell both Aunt Leslie and the policewoman. If I were left out in the forest the way I am now, I would become prey for the hunt. Wild bison would devour me. And I don't even have my amulets to protect me. I don't have Mom and Dad. I don't have the Hand of Fatima. I don't have Isabelle.

Isabelle was Baby A when we were womb-mates. That means she was the stronger one, the one with the greater chance of survival. After the doctor pried our fingers apart, it took him ninety seconds to pull out the rest of me. Isabelle was ninety seconds older and weighed four more ounces than I did at birth. Our weight difference has stayed pretty much the same since. Even if one of us spends a week in bed while the other one spends a week swimming, there's never more than half a pound difference between us. Still, it has always seemed like Isabelle is stronger than me.

Isabelle would have been very popular in the ancient world. Some great artist would have made a statue of her. In ancient Egypt, she would have been Nefertiti's friend. In ancient Greece, she would have been a Muse, a goddess of music.

I don't know how I even remember all this. I spend most of my time in art history class half listening and half sketching, drawing my classmates paying undivided attention.

In class, during slide shows, the dark, split only by a narrow beam of light, somehow lets people think they are alone. I sketch my friends scratching their armpits, fixing wedgies, and picking their noses, all in the presence of great art.

Even though he coaches our boys' basketball team, my art history teacher, Mr. Rhys, is barely five feet tall. He will jot down a few facts on the board, turn off the lights, then talk us through the slides, even though he could have easily used the classroom Smart Board. Peeking over his thick glasses, he often clears his throat between sentences, as if the dust the projector light catches on its way to the screen bothers him.

Every face in the class blurs now into the tiny tear bubbles that are welling into my eyes. And I know that I am not remembering, but somehow seeing something that is happening somewhere else, without me. Maybe this is like that levitating thing people talk about, that moving towards the light. Except I am moving back towards my old life.

My chair in the classroom is empty now.

Today Jean Michel Brun, my computer whiz, art history class crush, the boy with the big Afro, the boy with the radio announcer's voice, the boy I sometimes dream of moving to New York and going to art school with, and sharing a dirty paint-stained loft with, will be sitting in his usual seat, halfway between me and my best friend, Tina. Sometimes I spend the entire class watching him tug at the small gold loop earring in his right ear. It amazes me that he's not split his earlobe in two.

It amazes me, too, that Tina and I don't burn holes through his head with our stares.

I am a "smile if you get caught staring" kind of starer. I make eye contact. If I'm feeling bold, I might even wave. I also take my time looking away. And when I do, I look at the floor, then look back up and start staring again.

Tina is more a stealth admirer. She treats the whole thing like some kind of covert operation. She turns away immediately if she gets caught, then she starts tugging at her bra strap or patting down her straightened hair. Tina has an advantage over me. She and Jean Michel are also taking a computer science lab elective together.

Mr. Rhys's slide show now moves on to illuminated manuscripts, brightly painted books with gold lettering. I remember Isabelle telling me, "I'll take this class when they finally teach African art," and I momentarily lose interest in everything Mr. Rhys has to say. Now Italian frescoes mean nothing to me. But my sweet Leonardo and his *Mona Lisa* I still love, even while imagining my sister writing protest letters to Principal Volcy saying that, although our school was named after Toni Morrison, a great writer, we were not living up to her reputation or her legacy.

My presentation was going to be about my sister-approved art: Algerian rock paintings and *ibeji* statuettes, effigies of

Yoruba twins from Nigeria. I was also going to throw in some pictures of sequined vodou flags from Haiti, each thread, sequin, and bead shining like a tiny sun, Haiti's own illuminated manuscripts.

Isabelle was supposed to skip lunch and come listen to me do my presentation. She'd helped me prepare for it, printed articles, checked books out of the school media center.

But I am not there.

She is not there.

In the classroom where I'm longing to be, Mr. Rhys plows right through several centuries of art. He also goes on and on about depth perception, shadow and light, and movement and rest.

In the projector-illuminated dark, Jean Michel Brun waits until Tina's not looking, then he reaches over to hand me a note.

DO YOU WANT TO MEET LATER?

I peer down to read the note.

His words are all in capital letters, implying urgency.

Could he have figured out a way to pass a note to my ghost, sitting invisibly there in that classroom?

In the sunken-under dark, I imagine sitting next to Jean Michel in art history and life drawing classes in New York, at the New School, or NYU. We are no longer teenagers, but a young man and woman starting our lives together. Our adventure sounds like the description of an indie movie. *Two young* artists, in love, leave Florida to make it in New York's crazy, incestuous art world.

But back to the policewoman. What did she mean? *What happened was not exactly an accident.*

The policewoman's star keeps shining even behind my shut eyelids. It grows brighter and brighter until I can no longer see anything else.

I remember Mr. Rhys once saying, before lowering the shades and turning off the lights in his classroom, that there is more darkness in the world than light, more abysses than mountains, more invisible places than visible ones. Maybe he'd meant this in some artistic or philosophical way, but it might also be true in the real world.

Until the policewoman appeared with her star, I didn't realize that I was surrounded by both too much darkness and too much light. I was used to living two lives at once, sometimes carrying around in my head both Isabelle's memories and mine, both her dreams and mine. Sometimes I said "I" even when talking about the two of us, and I said "we" when I meant just me. I sometimes tasted what she was eating, especially when it was something with strawberries, which I don't like. The same thing happened to her, too. She hated onions, which I sometimes ate just to annoy her. But I don't remember ever seeing such a blinding star with her before.

I lie there wishing I could see rainbows and glories instead. But the policewoman's massive star is starting to block out every other possible thing. Her star looks like it's about to explode.

"She seems very agitated," I hear someone say.

It sounds like Aunt Leslie. It might also be the policewoman.

Then the star explodes.

A streak of red and orange bursts in a Russian doll series of fires before my eyes. I hear an alarm and a long beep, and all of a sudden the room feels crowded with not only more bodies but more voices. Something heavy and loud pounds into my chest, and every time it lands, I feel like I am being struck by lightning. The beep continues as the exploding star fades into darkness.

The tube in my throat is abruptly yanked out. I clench both my fists, then gasp. Coughing seems to offer the only relief. I cough up what seems like rivers, fishes, sea glass. I feel like I have been underwater for hours and am only allowed a few seconds on the surface. I need to take in as much air as I can before I sink under again. People are tugging at my arms, my legs. And someone unclenches one of my fists.

If I could, to stay on top, I would hold on to the side of the hospital bed, like an anchor, like a boat. But I can't. I am allowed only a few short breaths. I tighten my fist even harder.

But this time there's something in my hand. I didn't feel the hand that put it there. But the thing itself is sharp and cold against my palm. It is flat and attached to a string, a gold chain. It is my good luck charm, my Hand of Fatima from Aunt Leslie.

CHAPTER 3

I ONCE WROTE a story about a girl who could feel no pain, no hot or cold, no bruises, no pressure, absolutely no pain at all. Isabelle and I were in the ninth grade and I was researching unusual illnesses for a science project when I came across congenital insensitivity to pain.

Traces of this story now come to me as I sink deeper under, aided by whatever is being pumped into my veins.

When I was a baby, I never cried at all. When I was one and just learning to walk, I'd bump into things and not even wince. When I had my first ear infection at two, it didn't bother me at all.

It was the only time I had written myself on paper, even fictionally, as an only child. Sure, I had fantasized about it, imagining that I'd get two of everything if Isabelle wasn't there, twice as much of my parents' time and attention, twice the amount of clothes and toys.

Our parents never tried to morph us, though. The only time we dressed alike was when we played dress-up and turned ourselves into identical princesses. Otherwise we are wearing different outfits in all our childhood pictures. Even when friends and family members gave us matching dresses, Mom and Dad would make sure that we wore them on different days. We never merged our names, either (Gisabelle), like some twins do, even though we have identical voices, which are impossible to tell apart on the phone.

At school, Mom and Dad always asked that we be put in different classes so we could have our own sets of friends. They didn't want us to spend all of our school hours using twin speak. Over time we each developed our own interests. We tried, for the most part, to be our own people.

But now I don't even know how Isabelle is feeling. I don't even know whether she's alive. Our bodies were shaken up in different ways. Our minds might have been, too. I can't seem to stay focused on a single thought.

I'm turning into my namesake, Grandma Sandrine, before she died. Grandma Sandrine had forgotten Mom and Dad and Aunt Leslie, but occasionally she'd still remember Isabelle and me.

When she became sick, Grandma Sandrine, who'd been a nurse's aide most of her life, decided she was a painter. At first she was horrible at it, just randomly throwing paint on the canvas and trashing her apartment in the process. But eventually, her canvases started to make a little bit of sense. She stacked up more than twenty-five of them. Later, we found out that her sudden creative urges came from the fact that part of her brain—the prefrontal cortex—was disappearing. Even though it was taking away her memory, this disease had made her an artist, until she couldn't stand up or even sit up long enough to paint anymore.

Once, when she was super medicated, Grandma Sandrine told Isabelle and me that Haiti produced so many artists and so much art that the art spilled over into nature and traveled in people's veins. Grandma Sandrine just hadn't realized that she was one of those people with acrylics, oils, and a color palette in her blood.

Grandma Sandrine's canvases are now in our garage. Isabelle likes to say that it wasn't the brain disease or Grandma Sandrine's Haitian veins that gave her that final rush of creativity. It was knowing she was going to die. This finally released the artist who'd been trapped inside of her while she was raising Mom and Aunt Leslie on her own.

Isabelle knew before everyone else that Grandma Sandrine was going to die. Just as sitting in that car before the crash, each

of us knew, in our own way, that our little fortress was crumbling. Not in the way it turned out, but in some other way that
also seemed beyond repair. And now I'm learning that the person who'd shattered it meant to hurt us.

What can I tell the policewoman about that? Do I know
something, many things, that, as with Grandma Sandrine, have
slipped my mind?

I am trying very hard to hold on to the surface, trying hard
to keep my head above water, trying against all odds to remember. But if by chance I can't hold on, if by chance I can't surface,
I wonder if Grandma Sandrine will be at the other end of things,
waiting for me. Will Isabelle? Mom and Dad?

The day of Grandma Sandrine's funeral, I found one of
Isabelle's short stories next to the sink, in the bathroom she
and I share. At the top of the page, Isabelle had scribbled
with a red marker, "To Be Put to Music One Day."

The story was called "The Language of the Palms."

> *On a lovely green block, two identical palm*
> *trees (Palm A and Palm B) often whispered*
> *to one another, especially when there was a*
> *breeze. Sometimes the people on the street*
> *could hear them whooshing in the wind, but*
> *since the people didn't speak the language of the*
> *palms, they didn't understand what they were*

saying. One day, the palms switched places, and
no one noticed . . .

Isabelle never got to put those words to music. She either lost
interest or discovered that she couldn't.

Am I remembering all of this alone? Or is Isabelle remembering with me?

CHAPTER 4

PAIN, SO MUCH pain.

Flesh exploding pain.

Pins and needles pain.

Fiery hot pain.

Cold pain.

Hammer pounding on your head pain.

Hammer pounding on your bones pain.

Star-blinding pain.

Pain that makes it impossible to even scream.

The most *painful* thing about this kind of pain is that you never know how long it's going to last. Somehow, when you're right in the middle of it, your whole body feels locked in, as though the pain is going to last forever.

I want to be under, way under, in a dark but pain-free world. In a class full of beautiful paintings and beautiful boys. I want to be at all sixteen of the birthday parties that Isabelle and I have had, at all the wonderful vacations we've had with our parents, at all the first days of school, at all the church services, even the ones we found so boring. At all the swimming and tennis classes, at all the art and creative writing camps. I want to be home with Mom and Dad and Isabelle and Dessalines. I want to be back in my life, even when it was starting to fall apart.

I'm in a different room when I wake up this time. This room has a bunch of glass bricks on the wall, filtering the light through.

I catch a word, a phrase, here and there. *Heart rate. Blood pressure.* Even though I'm not always sure where it's coming from. The words begin to merge like a song. *Heart rate. Blood pressure. Lazarus.*

"Lazarus" doesn't fit somehow until I realize that our minister, Pastor Ben, must have come through at some point when I was under. The only thing Pastor Ben likes more than his cotton guayabera shirts is to pull on his long white beard and talk about Lazarus.

Pastor Ben's eggplant-colored face, with the shock of silver hair that tops it and the matching silver beard that frames it, swings in and out of my view.

I hear him say something about twenty-four hours, then Lazarus. Has it been twenty-four hours already? Is he calling *me* Lazarus? After the man who came back from the dead? Wasn't there ever a girl who came back from the dead? A set of twins? An entire family?

I can't remember now the last time I saw Pastor Ben. It might have been the Sunday before.

Or the one before that.

On the most recent Sunday, Dad was away, so we skipped church. Mom didn't like the idea of showing up at church just the three of us, without Dad.

Mom, Isabelle, and I had the croque-madame special at Café de l'Amour, the French bistro near our house. Then we went to the Bass Museum on Miami Beach to see an exhibit of pentimento paintings.

I remember the day Mr. Rhys introduced our class to pentimento paintings. I fell in love immediately. Beyond the image on the surface of the painting, there was also an old image you could still see. It was as if the artist wanted you to know that nothing came out perfect. Something had been there first, then had been erased, though not all the way.

In Italian, *pentimento* means "repentance," Mr. Rhys had told us. In painting over his or her old work, the artist was not just *repainting*, but also *repenting*.

Because I knew they would love it, too, I spat out all this

information to Mom and Isabelle at the Bass Museum that Sunday afternoon. They were just as excited as I was, looking for buried images in the paintings.

Mom said that the paintings were playing hide-and-seek with us. *Kash kash liben*, as she called it in Creole. In some cases, the top image had nearly disappeared and what was underneath, the under drawing, became the main painting. Other times, the images merged, creating something totally unexpected.

An elephant crawling out of someone's heart.

A woman's face as a tombstone.

Lazarus. Lazarus. Lazarus.

Pastor Ben must have been standing there in the room with the glass bricks, saying something to me.

Now Aunt Leslie, the policewoman with the star on her chest, Pastor Ben, Mom, Dad, and Isabelle are all pentimento.

If I could paint a bunch of pentimento paintings, they would show Aunt Leslie sobbing while standing on top of the policewoman's star. They would show Pastor Ben praying for me to a God that I could probably reach out and touch now, since I feel so far from actual people, and so close to the unknown. They would show me and Isabelle and Mom and Dad inside Dad's SUV. My pentimento paintings would all show me with the people I love, slipping in and out of view, with people who are trying hard to hold on to me while I'm fighting not to let go.

In the hospital room, I try to take in as much as I can. Before I slip under, I hear someone say that I was moved out of the Pediatric Intensive Care Unit because I have a concussion but no life-threatening internal injuries, no broken bones. Then all those other injuries—the fractures, the contusions and lacerations, the tube, the missing teeth—must have been Isabelle's and hers alone.

Once, when we were around five or six, a much bigger (and dumber) park playmate shoved us together so he could "mash us into one person." Before our parents could intervene, Isabelle threw her body in front of mine and said, superhero-like, "Don't worry, Giz, I'll protect you." She then returned the boy's shove, made a fist, reached up, and punched the boy smack in the middle of his chin. In her mind, Isabelle always had to stand between me and danger.

Seems like she had protected me again.

The things I do remember are what's keeping me on the surface. Happy or sad, these memories are mine. They are what I want to go back to when I am well again. If I am ever truly well again. This must also be true for Isabelle. How could it not be? Our lives began with one cell. We are almost the same person. So if I am alive, she must be, too.

At least the pain is dying down. On a scale from one million to a billion—as Dr. Rosemay, our pediatrician, used to ask

Isabelle and me before going to the usual one to ten range—I went from about a billion to a million.

Sometimes, lying there, I hear the faint sound of a female newscaster, either coming from the nurses' station, or from one of the rooms nearby. The occasional between-stations static makes it sound more like a radio than a TV. I try to concentrate on the calm, even-toned newscaster's voice to hear whether something will be said about my family or me. I only learn that it is Saturday night, eighty degrees, partly cloudy, with a 25 percent chance of showers.

The next time I'm awake, the male nurse who's checking my IV stops now and then to look at the glass bricks on the walls. He has a scratchy voice even as he is mumbling to himself. And it seems that I'm drifting off again, because all of a sudden, I feel his hand on the tips of my fingers and he's gently shaking them the way someone might nudge a person who's nodding off in class, or at church.

"Isabelle." He calls me by my sister's name. "Try to keep those eyes open."

I open my mouth out of shock, but it must seem to him like I am yawning. Some drool drips past the side of my mouth and makes it onto the front of my hospital gown. The rest he quickly catches with a napkin, and I can't help but feel very small, like a baby.

My mouth does have teeth. I still have all my teeth.

"Isabelle." The male nurse says it again. Then I realize that he thinks I'm my sister. He thinks I'm Isabelle.

This has happened to me all my life, but nowhere and at no time is it more important not to be mistaken for Isabelle. At no time is it more important for her to be her. And for me to be me.

He thinks I am Isabelle. How do I tell him who I am when no words are coming out of my mouth?

I wish he'd say something else. Something clarifying like "Keep your eyes open and stay alive because your family is alive and is waiting for you." Or "Keep your eyes closed because you're the only one left." Why won't he just explain everything to me? I can't ask. The crash has taken my voice away. And now this nurse thinks I am Isabelle. Does Aunt Leslie think so, too?

Maybe I'm the one who's all turned around and I actually am Isabelle. Maybe it's all part of having this concussion. How do I even know for sure that I'm not Isabelle?

I look down and try to move my arms. They are as black and blue as a stormy sky. I try to clench my jaws as the nurse wipes more drool off my face.

I want my body to be a life raft back to my family, and back to my sister, the real Isabelle, who may be somewhere out there, wounded, worried, confused. Just like I am.

CHAPTER 5

AUNT LESLIE'S BACK. This time she's not wearing her doctor's coat. Instead, she's crying. Her body's shaking, unable to remain still. Her pretty fingernails are down to nubs.

Usually I would praise my own attention to detail, but there are no details. Only large, massive things are happening. The way Aunt Leslie's mumbling to herself, though, makes me feel like we'd been talking for a while and I've forgotten some of the things she's said.

Aunt Leslie has always known Isabelle and me so well. She's even wearing our favorite color, an indigo blue dress with sheer short sleeves. She's beautiful, like Mom is beautiful, but in a more reserved way. When they were little, people used to call her and Mom *"les bonnes soeurs,"* or "the nuns."

All that crying could not be for me alone. She must know that I would know this. I breathe in her expensive lavender-scented perfume as she walks over to the bed. I'm surprised I can still smell. I'm glad I can still see, though my head feels too heavy to move.

My whole body can't move. I can't speak, but I can see Aunt Leslie and the glass bricks on the walls. Seeing the filtered light form a halo around her reminds me of her early sixteenth birthday present to Isabelle and me, a trip to a monarch butterfly sanctuary with her and Mom and Dad.

The monarch sanctuary was high in the mountains of Central Mexico, at the entrance to a pine forest, full of butterfly-covered fir and eucalyptus trees. Isabelle and I had always been fascinated by monarch butterflies. Most of our elementary and middle school projects were about them. But when we got near the butterfly trees, the flapping wings sounded like buzz saws in our ears and we both started sneezing nonstop, scaring hundreds of them away.

The Aztecs, whose land we were standing on, believed that the monarch butterflies were the spirits of dead children returned to life. It was all too much for us to take up close.

Back at the bed-and-breakfast where we were staying, we both broke out in hives all over our arms and legs.

"Thank God we have a doctor with us," Mom said.

It turned out we weren't the first people to be allergic to a monarch typhoon. The B&B had everything from EpiPens to Benadryl. Aunt Leslie prescribed Benadryl.

Later that night, even after taking the Benadryl, we couldn't fall asleep. When Isabelle finally did, I dreamed that I'd turned into a butterfly-covered fir. Isabelle did, too. We'd both been so excited about the trip and the possibility of seeing all the butterflies. Our monarch fantasies had turned into nightmares.

When we woke up the next morning, we were already on to our next favorite thing in the guidebook, another one of our common passions: cathedrals. We asked to visit one of our grandfather's favorite places, the sixteenth-century cathedrals of Guanajuato, a wish that, given our blisters and swollen faces, Aunt Leslie and our parents were happy to oblige.

We liked the cathedrals a lot more than the monarchs. We liked the way the outside towers loomed over us, as though they were built to make the rest of the world feel small. We liked the way the light traveled through the stained-glass windows to create a golden glow. We liked the hundreds of tiny candles, each representing a person's deepest desires. We liked watching people bow, then cross themselves, then dab their faces with a bit of holy water, the water of life. We liked wowing Mom and Dad and Aunt Leslie with everything Grandpa

Marcus had taught us about cathedrals. We liked experiencing all of this together.

In the hospital room, my necklace is now hanging on a tack on the dark green wall across from me.

Is it Sunday morning?

What was this thing they always said on all the police shows? The more time passes without news, the more likely an outcome you don't want to have.

"Isabelle," Aunt Leslie says. "I know you have many questions."

So Aunt Leslie does think I'm Isabelle.

I'm not Isabelle, I want to scream. I am Giselle.

Though why does it even matter?

It seems as if she's going to tell me something important. Like maybe she will finally tell me about my family.

"Isabelle," she says, the melodic voice and her lavender perfume blending into some worldly "je ne sais quoi" irresistible essence that one day I want to have.

"Isabelle . . . don't want . . . worry . . . parents . . . because . . . okay," I hear her say.

I'm not catching every word immediately. The words must travel a little, then echo back before they fully sink in. I have to piece them together. Otherwise they'll all be lost like so many words must have already been lost on me. So many doctors' visits. Pastor Ben's visits and who knows who else.

So I don't have to worry about my parents, because they're okay? But why haven't they come to see me?

"Know . . . wondering . . . where . . . you are?"

You bet I'm wondering where I am, I want to say.

"Children's wing . . . Jackson. Parents . . . same hospital . . . across . . . the bridge . . . adult wing."

So I am still in Miami. My parents are in the same hospital but across some kind of bridge. She must mean across the walkway, the one that joins the adult part of the hospital to the children's wing. Either Mom or Dad drives us under that walkway almost every single day on our way to and from school. I never thought of it before as a possible lifeline, a bridge, between wounded parents and their children.

I imagine Aunt Leslie saying similar things to my parents. Thinking that I am Isabelle, she'd probably say, "David, Sylvie, I don't want you to worry about Isabelle."

But what about the real Isabelle?

Aunt Leslie's moving away, the scent, the voice slipping away without her saying anything about Isabelle.

And that's when I know.

She doesn't have to say it.

Isabelle is gone.

Isabelle is dead.

Maybe it's because things are becoming clearer, but I can hear her more clearly, too, even as she moves farther away from me and begins to cry again.

"Oh my God, oh my God!" Her head is bobbing up and down. Her words sound like real pleas to God, not just declarations of her astonishment.

My sister, Isabelle, is dead. And somehow everyone's thinking that I am her. So they're thinking I'm dead.

"Isabelle," Aunt Leslie is saying now. She's slipping back into doctor mode. "They did everything possible for Giselle. Just like they did for you and your parents. But she had some terrible head and neck injuries. She was broken."

Too broken for me to even feel?

I'm now grateful for the day or two that I didn't know the truth. But now Aunt Leslie thinks knowing the truth is better.

I can't even cry. I can't make tears. But rather than wanting to coil up in a ball—something I couldn't physically do anyway—rather than wanting to stay there and die, rather than wanting to close my eyes and sink deeper under, I imagine myself shedding my own skin and walking away to wherever Isabelle is and holding her hand.

How could I not have known? Maybe I didn't want to know. Maybe I needed to not know.

"Isabelle." Aunt Leslie is standing with her back to me. Too sad, maybe, to look at me. She's looking at the glass bricks on the wall.

I can tell from the way some tree branches sway behind the glass that right outside are treetops, green, healthy treetops. We are on the second or third floor of the building. There is a world outside. Sun. Trees. Clouds. People are going about their lives, just as we had been. They're thinking that nothing bad can ever happen to them.

I am now in some place that feels like the VIP section of the hospital ward, a place that, if I knew exactly where I was, might signal to me that I am already getting better. And hearing Aunt Leslie call me by my sister's name is now comforting me. As long as everyone thinks that Isabelle is me, then Isabelle is also getting better. She is still here, in this room, in the world.

"I'm so sorry, Izzie," Aunt Leslie says with her back still turned to me.

I can tell that she's on the verge of telling me more that she's not supposed to. The way she told Isabelle and me about sex some years back, about it being something that happened between a man and a woman, rather than between bees and birds. We were nine years old then and were mostly unsure of what she was talking about. But somehow we couldn't imagine our father pollinating our mother, either.

Aunt Leslie is about to become my confidante again. I can feel it. She walks back to my bedside, then grabs my hand. She holds on too tight, but I welcome her grip. I don't want her to let go.

"Izzie," she says. "You're in there, I can tell. When you wake up, you'll be okay. You just have to try a little bit harder now."

This sounds more like a wish than a medical opinion. She seems to be hoping that lying here with a bruised brain is all that is wrong with me, that I will be myself again as soon as I wake up. But why wake up when Isabelle won't be here?

I will never see Isabelle again, except maybe when I look in the mirror and pretend, just as everyone is saying, that I am her, and she is me. Who would I be? Who *could* I be without her? Who would I watch different versions of *Little Women* with?

"I'm to be a famous musician myself, and all creation is to rush to hear me." We would always shout along with whichever actor was playing Laurie.

Then Jo: *"I want to do something splendid before I go . . . and mean to astonish you all someday."*

We didn't need to say these lines out loud. We both knew that's how Isabelle felt, that's who she wanted to be, someone who would do something incredible one day, someone who would put words, pictures, feelings to music in a way that no one had ever done before, someone who would astonish the world.

I will never see her put her crazy, unfinished fables to music. I will never again hear her talk about the types of music that few kids our age were into: strings, jazz, new age, opera. How could I even be here when she is gone? How could I not have felt her leaving me?

Maybe she died in the car before they pulled us out? Maybe she died when her head hit the side window? When the flute case kept banging into her?

"Isabelle, you're very lucky," Aunt Leslie is saying now. Ever the doctor again. She's giving me information, telling me things to encourage me, to help me wake up.

Lucky?

How could I be lucky?

Lucky would be to have Isabelle with me.

"Pastor Ben's right," she adds. "You're going to wake up. Like Lazarus."

Science is her anchor, but when it comes to family she'll take faith. She'll take Lazarus. Between my sister and me, I am Lazarus. I have returned from the dead.

But what good was returning from the dead without Isabelle?

"I can't wait to see what kind of women you two turn out to be," Dad would randomly exclaim now and then.

Neither one of us knew what kind of women we were going to be. And now Isabelle will never become a woman at all.

I want to become a woman. I *have* to become a woman. Not just for me, but for Isabelle, too. But my head feels too heavy now. My body is much weaker than my will. I sink under again.

It's the only way I know to escape all this, to avoid having another star explode in my head.

It's the only way I know to avoid this other kind of pain, the kind for which if I was asked for a number and a level of agony, I would say a sextillion.

CHAPTER 6

LAST CHRISTMAS, MOM and Dad went on a couple's holiday cruise to Alaska and dropped Isabelle and me off at Uncle Patrick's, in New York, for the week between Christmas and New Year's. Uncle Patrick isn't married but has a longtime girlfriend, a music producer named Alejandra. They live in a twelfth-floor loft in Brooklyn, in a neighborhood called Dumbo, which is short for Down Under the Manhattan Bridge Overpass. Their building used to be an old paint factory, and from their wraparound wall-to-ceiling windows, you can see the Brooklyn and Manhattan Bridges, as well as the East River and a nearby park.

Half-buried in the cobblestoned streets outside their building are railroad tracks, which were once used by a local train to carry merchandise from the river to some old factories.

"That was a long time ago," Uncle Patrick told us when we arrived, "before people like us moved in. Back then the immigrants were factory workers, not owners here."

Still, Uncle Patrick is very proud of the apartment. He loves New York more than any city in the world, even Port-au-Prince, where he was born and which he left with Dad when they were teenagers.

Uncle Patrick had discovered a once-famous rap duo called the Expats, which is made up of a Haitian American brother and sister. The Expats had been most famous when Isabelle and I were little, too young to appreciate their sound or the strong political messages for which they were known.

"They were basically doing the same thing your dad's been doing since he left the army and started studying law," Uncle Patrick told us. "They were defending the rights of immigrants."

During that visit, Uncle Patrick gave us yet another tour of his place—we got a tour each time we went there—and showed us some more recent Expats posters in his home office.

Throughout our stay, we listened nonstop to both of the Expats albums. Their sound was a mix of lively Haitian *konpa*, reggae, and hip-hop. Though I loved the Expats, Isabelle didn't like their music.

"They're no Emeline," she said, citing her favorite bluesy Haitian singer.

During our week in New York, Alejandra was visiting her family in Venezuela, so Isabelle and I saw a lot of New York City with Uncle Patrick. He took us to the Empire State Building to see the city from up high, and, in spite of the cold, we spent hours standing in front of the store windows along Fifth Avenue. We visited the Christmas tree in Rockefeller Center, which seemed like it was a hundred feet tall. Then we went ice-skating, or "ice-falling," as Isabelle called it, in the packed skating rink beneath the plaza. We had front-row seats at the Rockettes show at Radio City Music Hall and to *The Nutcracker* at Lincoln Center.

We even sat in on a recording session for an up-and-coming group that Uncle Patrick was working with, a multinational teen girl a cappella group he told us was going to be huge but that we'd not heard anything about since.

Our favorite memory, though, was of the New Year's Eve blizzard. We had never seen so much snow in our entire lives. The snow had begun falling while we were asleep and by the time we woke up, there were a couple of feet of it on the ground.

We went out in front of Uncle Patrick's building, played snow baseball and made snow angels. Our parents called later that morning as we were thawing out in Uncle Patrick's apartment. Standing between the two of us, Uncle Patrick looked down at the city blanketed with snow, then at our awestruck faces, and told our parents, "I have never seen them happier."

But now Uncle Patrick is standing in this room with the glass bricks on the wall. He's standing there looking down at me in the hospital bed. Alejandra—with her baby face and high cheekbones combo that Uncle Patrick said won him over—is beside him, and they're both looking down at me with their penny-colored faces. They look like they want to cry.

I wish I was still sitting on Uncle Patrick's living room couch under a thick wool blanket as he, Isabelle, and I watched the television news on mute and tried to guess, from the words and images in the little box next to the anchor's head, what the news anchor was talking about. Whenever Alejandra was around, we'd pretend we were voice-over artists while watching nature documentaries, and out of all of us, Alejandra—her voice throaty and well paced—had the best documentary voice.

"I've never seen her so sad," Uncle Patrick is now saying on the phone while looking down at me on the hospital bed.

Who is he talking to? Is it Aunt Leslie? Dad? Mom?

I wish I could talk to Uncle Patrick. I wish he could hear me.

When Uncle Patrick gets off the phone, he walks closer to my face and puts the phone in front of it. The glare from the phone is so bright it reminds me of all the penlights, which are constantly being beamed into my eyes by the different head doctors. I do my best to concentrate, squinting to see better.

Does he want me to say something to the person on the other end of the phone?

He's trying to show me a picture on his screen.

The screen makes my eyes feel so hot that the light seems to be burning through them, but on it is a close-up of Dad's post-crash face, which I really want to see.

Dad's face is turned sideways, so I can only make out one side. From the profile, I can tell that his face is still kind of round, except now his cheeks are drooping a little around his cheekbones. There are little marks, too, all over his cheek, as if it had been poked with an ice pick in half a dozen places. Many of the little dots still look raw, like they've just been bleeding. This is probably from the shattered glass, the hundreds of tiny pieces of it that kept coming at us in the car. Small and large specks of glass were flying at us from every direction. At one point, I had to close my eyes. I suppose some of the glass landed on Dad's face.

I must have avoided some of it because even though I can't touch my face, I don't feel what I imagine I might feel if pieces of glass had been buried under my skin. I imagine my face might feel itchy if it had been full of glass. But I am out so much that maybe my face looks exactly like Dad's and I don't know it. Maybe even Dad doesn't realize that his face, or at least half of it, looks like a pincushion.

I wish I could see a picture of Dad's body. Can he walk? Can he talk? Can he call my name? Isabelle's name? Mom's name? Does he remember us?

Mom's face looks a little bit worse when Uncle Patrick switches to her picture. She's looking straight into the camera, though. Her head is shaved on one side and there's a line of stitches across her forehead, about twelve or fifteen of them. A few curls hang where her corkscrew twists used to be, making it look like she's sporting a Mohawk. She looks as if her forehead has been sewn back together by a mad scientist, like she's the Bride of Frankenstein.

Aren't they all mad scientists here, though? These doctors and their students in their white coats and pink and blue scrubs. I am starting to think of them as ducks and ducklings. There are many different ways of putting people back together. They seem to have put Mom back together with staples and stitches.

I had stitches before, once, after tumbling down the steep staircase by the gym at school. I'd cut my forehead four stitches' worth. While lying there at the bottom of the staircase, waiting for the school nurse to come, I panicked and thought I was going to die. There was so much blood on the floor next to me, I thought there was none left in my head.

"It looks worse than it is," the nurse said once she cleaned me up. "These kinds of cuts produce a lot of blood."

But she thought it serious enough to call my parents and have them meet me in the ER, where I would have a head scan.

"Can you get my sister?" I asked the nurse.

I knew that seeing Isabelle would be like seeing a calmer, unwounded version of myself, and that would reassure me.

"I'm still prettier than you," I joked to Isabelle after a plastic surgeon, at Mom's insistence, had meticulously sewn up my cut so that it basically healed scarless.

Later, Isabelle told Mom and Dad that she knew I'd be okay when I made my first silly remark about being prettier than her.

If things had turned out even a little differently, we all might crack jokes about Mom's picture, telling her that at least the Bride of Frankenstein had nice waves in her hair. But all I could think of were the stitches across her forehead.

Uncle Patrick wants me to know that my parents are alive. These pictures must have been taken just for me so I could see them, so I could know they're still alive.

Soon, Uncle Patrick begins clicking away, too, at my face. I can't tell what angle he's aiming for, but I think he's trying to show me in the best light. He wants them to see the best of me.

He then turns the phone around so I can see myself. My face looks as puffy and uneven as a deflating blimp. My eyes look tiny, my skin ashy. I don't want to see any more. I close my tiny eyes. I feel like I'm looking at a stranger. Some third person who no longer looks like me or Isabelle.

"Proof of life," they call it in the kidnapping movies. Uncle Patrick is trying to get proof of life. But there will be no proof of life for Isabelle.

Uncle Patrick doesn't call me by anyone's name, so I can't tell who he thinks I am. But there are no pictures of Isabelle for me to see.

CHAPTER 7

ISABELLE AND I used to want to be detectives when we were younger. We wanted to be like Nancy Drew, going around the world solving crimes.

Now I need amateur detective skills to solve the mystery of my own body. But what I know best is not all the medical jargon, but Isabelle, Mom and Dad, and home. And Dessalines.

Poor Dessalines. I hope Aunt Leslie and Uncle Patrick have found him.

Isabelle was the one who thought we should take in newborn Dessalines after his owner, one of Dad's clients, lost his asylum case and was deported to Pakistan. Isabelle wanted us to take in the whole litter, as well as the mother, but they were adopted by different people in Dad's office.

I wonder if Dessalines will understand that Isabelle, like his Dad's client, has also left him behind. Has he ever been able to tell Izzie and me apart? How will he react when she doesn't come home? Will he jump on me, claw my eyes out, peel my skin off, and try to find Isabelle underneath?

No, I don't understand the small chance of permanent brain damage that I hear the doctor discuss with the dozen or so medical students who walk in and out behind him. I keep hoping each time they poke the bottom of my feet that my toes will wriggle. I keep wishing I could scream, to either give them some hope or make them stop.

The head doctor writes some things down on his iPad, the iPad that holds my file—Isabelle's file—and he leads the pack out and they follow him like he's the mother duck and they are ducklings, terrified of getting lost.

After they leave me, I imagine them sitting in a conference room somewhere and talking in heavy medical jargon, about my toes and how they couldn't make them move. Or maybe they're saying that it's going to be impossible to ever make my toes move. Or maybe I'm misunderstanding all of this. Maybe they'll say that I have "turned the tide," that I'm better.

Before nightfall, the duck and ducklings gather near my head on the hour, it seems. And my eyes travel from one duckling's face to the next. The ducklings, the baby doctors, all look so eager, so young. They look only a few years older than Isabelle and me.

Every now and then Aunt Leslie stands there with the ducklings, next to the head duck. Then they walk out of the room together, ahead of everyone else. I feel like a prisoner in one of those movies where someone is being tortured but has to hide it when the congressional delegation comes to visit. Who do I whisper "Help" to if Aunt Leslie has joined them? Who do I pass my SOS note to, saying I want out?

I do want out of this unmoving body. I do want out of this place. I do want my life back. I want my parents back. I want my sister back.

Why haven't my parents come to see me? Maybe they're pinned to a bed, while doctors keep coming through. They, too, might be wondering when their toes will wiggle in a way that will make everyone happy. Or maybe they're also hoping that their voices will surprise them and actually be heard by the doctors who keep asking when they walk in the room, "How are we doing today?"

In my case they keep asking, "How are we doing today, Isabelle?"

I AM NOT ISABELLE.

I AM GISELLE!

How can I let them know that I'm not Isabelle? Or what if I am Isabelle and don't realize it? What if I'm the one who's wrong? What if I'm the one who's confused?

No, I don't fully understand all the medical jargon, but I still know some very Giselle things. These are things I think a lot about, but that Isabelle wouldn't give a second thought to, if she didn't invade my brain sometimes.

I force myself to remember how much the earth weighs— 6.6 sextillion short tons. I think of the names of at least twenty-five of the presidents that came before the current president of the United States. Trying to remember the Pythagorean theorem makes my brain throb. I also retreat to mental pictures of things I've drawn, most of which I've saved in sketch pads at home.

Many of my sketch pads are filled with drawings of my family, especially of Isabelle, either playing her flute or swimming. Looking at Isabelle made my body feel a lot less mysterious to me. It was my only way of knowing what my body looks like not just from front and back, but from every possible angle. Having her with me also meant having a kind of loudspeaker for my thoughts, even before they came to me.

The week before the crash, Dad was in Honduras interviewing people for some asylum cases his law firm was working on. Mom, Isabelle, and I were standing in the cereal aisle in the middle of the Publix supermarket near our house in Midtown Miami when Mom suddenly began to cry.

At home, while we were putting the groceries away, we heard Mom still sobbing on the phone. She was talking to Tina's mom,

Mrs. Marshall, who is a social worker and thus very used to hysterics.

"It's all beyond my comprehension," Mom told Mrs. Marshall. "I thought I was doing okay."

We unpacked all the groceries while Mom sat at the kitchen table near the sliding door that overlooked the backyard. In the dark, we couldn't see the pool or the garden that Mom and Dad had planted together, the banana and papaya trees, and the row of sugarcane near the date palm, mango, avocado trees, and flower beds.

When she hung up with Mrs. Marshall, Mom stumbled over to the bedroom she and Dad had shared, before he'd moved into one of the guest rooms. She hadn't made the bed since he left and wouldn't let Josiane, our cleaning lady, make it, either.

Mom climbed on top of the crumpled sheets and curled herself into a ball.

"What am I doing?" Mom asked Isabelle and me, while pulling a dirty sheet over her head.

Dad called us that night from Honduras. Still lying in the unmade bed, Mom smiled from ear to ear, pretending she was okay. At times during the conversation, she lowered her voice to say some things to him that she didn't want us to hear. Other times, she stayed quiet to listen to what he had to say.

Isabelle and I got in the bed with Mom and pressed our ears

against her chest to listen to her heart's reaction to whatever it was that Dad was saying.

"I spoke to Vee," Mom told him.

Mrs. Marshall's first name was Vera, but both my parents called her Vee.

"Vee still thinks we're making a big mistake again," Mom said.

She then handed the phone to Isabelle and said, "Go ahead, girls, say a few words to your father."

Before they'd announced their separation, whenever Dad was away, it was always a struggle to pull the phone away from Mom, but that night she wanted to end the conversation quickly.

When it was our turn to speak to Dad, Isabelle put the phone on speaker. We listened for the hurt in Dad's voice, yet his voice was strong and firm, just as it's always been.

"How are you and your sister really doing?" he asked.

Isabelle and I were both angry at him.

"How do you think we're doing?" Isabelle snapped. She wasn't just speaking for us at that moment, she was also speaking for Mom.

"Girls!" Mom called out, as though she could read both our minds.

Isabelle and I had both hoped to make Dad feel too guilty to leave us for good.

"You were both way out of line," Mom shouted, even though I hadn't said a word.

"No, you and Dad are out of line," I shouted back.

That night, Isabelle and I slept in the unmade bed with Mom. We tried to get used to the idea that it would eventually be just the three of us in the house. The only thing we were wrong about was just which three it would be.

In the car, while driving us to school the next morning, Mom looked like she was already at the end of her day. Her white T-shirt was wrinkled and her jeans had quarter-size lipstick smudges from one of her jobs at the local TV station where she made up the anchors' faces. Still, she managed to give us each a quick forehead kiss before we ran inside the school.

I felt like sneaking out of the building and skipping school that day. I was about to ask Isabelle to play hooky and come to the movies with me, like we'd done a few times, but one of the hall monitors noticed us and called out, "You're late! You're late!"

Isabelle and I waved goodbye to each other before running down the hall in opposite directions.

When I got to my homeroom, everyone was already seated and Madame Blaise, who doubles as both my homeroom and French teacher, was taking attendance. Isabelle's friend Lois, who sits at the desk in front of me, was doing last-minute homework and chewing her gum way too loud. Lois is first chair for flute in the school orchestra. Isabelle is second flute. Lois and Isabelle have been friends since we were in middle school.

"Giselle, *t'es en retard*," Madame Blaise called from behind her desk at the front of the room. Just as she might even if I were to show up now in my hospital gown.

Madame Blaise was the only teacher who pronounced my name like it was meant to be pronounced. She pronounced it Jee-Zell, rather than Jay-Zale, the way almost everyone else did. Madame Blaise once told me that *Giselle*, the ballet about a peasant girl who loses the man she loves, then dies of a broken heart, was one of her favorites.

Mom and Dad had taken Isabelle and me to see that ballet one summer when we were visiting Uncle Patrick in New York. We've seen pictures of ourselves sitting in our front-row seats, Isabelle in a pink, rose-petal-hemmed ballerina dress and me in a burgundy one. We both held our programs up for the camera. Neither of us remembers seeing the ballet. We might have slept through it. We were four years old.

Isabelle and I once looked up her name in a baby book. Next to her name were the words "loyal to God."

"With a name like that, I should be a nun," she said.

Here we were, the one who didn't like dance named for a brokenhearted dancer and the one who was supposed to be faithful, standing on the margins between faith and disbelief.

We might have even been looking at her name in the baby book when she said that she was standing on the margins between faith and disbelief.

"Where'd you hear that?" I asked her. "And what does it mean anyway?"

"It means we can believe whatever we want," she said.

After graduating from middle school, Isabelle and I decided to make a time capsule. We bought a plastic storage bin with a tight lid and filled it with all kinds of things, including our school caps and gowns and diplomas.

"What are we going to use middle school diplomas for anyway?" she said.

We also put in copies of family pictures from the time we were babies, copies of pictures of our parents holding us before we could walk on our own, both of them looking equally sleep deprived and exhausted.

We threw in some old CDs of our favorite songs—everything we used to blast in our rooms: rhythm and blues and hip-hop for me, and world music, gospel, and classical for Isabelle. We also put in some of the books we loved, the Nancy Drew mysteries, Toni Morrison's *The Bluest Eye*, *Frankenstein*, *Little Women*, and *Alice in Wonderland*.

I made a sketch of the two of us swimming, and we took the extra step of putting that in a plastic bag and pressing it between our copies of *Seventeen* and *Essence* magazines. We were also supposed to write letters to the future.

Dear Future, mine began.

My name is Giselle and I am a twin. My twin's name is Isabelle. My parents' names are David and Sylvie Boyer. My best friend's name is Tina Marshall.

Boring stuff.

Dear Future, Isabelle's read.

Please stun me.

Astound me.

Flabbergast me.

Delight me.

Amaze me.

Astonish me!

She also copied a few pages from her journal, a series of short "To Be Put to Music One Day" entries I was never allowed to see.

On the container lid, she wrote with a fat permanent marker, "Not to be opened until the year 3000, when Isabelle and Giselle Boyer are long gone."

That night while our parents were asleep, we went outside and with their gardening shovels dug a hole big enough to actually bury our time capsule, not just put it in the ground with a layer of dust on top.

I want to believe that I can go home, sneak out of bed, and

feel my way through the dark with Isabelle next to me. We'd pick up our parents' shovels and dig up the dirt, still muddy from the sprinklers. This time, we wouldn't muffle our laughter or dive behind the bushes when the motion sensor lights came on. And her hands would still be there to reach for me when my feet would catch on weeds or vines.

But I couldn't dig up that time capsule anyway. It was buried deeper into the earth by the construction people when our pool was put in a couple of years ago.

CHAPTER 8

I THINK I'M dreaming when Mom and Dad are wheeled into the hospital room the next day. The bed is raised to what I've started calling the daytime half-sitting angle when Mom comes through the door. Then Dad.

Aunt Leslie is pushing Mom's wheelchair and Uncle Patrick is pushing Dad's. Both Mom and Dad are wearing hospital gowns, matching light blue ones, just like the one I have on. Mom is sitting with her feet resting on the wheelchair's footplates.

Dad's left leg is stretched out in front of him, a cast rising from his ankle to slightly above the knee and another one from his left shoulder down to his wrist. He is most hurt on his left side, where the car slammed into us. Isabelle was sitting behind him. Mom and I, it seems, were on the good side, or at least the better side, of things.

Mom edges forward as if to jump out of the chair, but instead she nearly folds in two, and when she raises her head again she's grimacing in pain.

Dad motions for Uncle Patrick to push his chair next to hers, and Dad reaches out and uses his good hand to take Mom's hand in his, in a way that reminds me of how they used to hold hands when Isabelle and I were little, almost like they didn't even realize they were doing it. Maybe it's because they're upright now, but they don't look as bad as they did in the pictures. Dad's face is not a pincushion after all. Mom's buzz cut looks just as bad. Her forehead is covered with a bandage the size of a dollar bill.

Mom looks over at Dad and he holds her gaze, too, and a million words seem to flow between them, at a speed and in a language that no one else in the room can possibly understand. Their way of communicating is a lot like Isabelle's and mine. Speaking out loud isn't always necessary. A single touch, a glance from Dad can always calm Mom down.

"You have to avoid sudden movements like that. Your bruised ribs can't take all that yet," Aunt Leslie tells Mom.

Mom's main issue seems to be the cut across her forehead and her bruised ribs. Based on the plaster, it looks like Dad's left arm and leg are broken.

"Are you ready?" Uncle Patrick asks Dad.

Dad tries very hard to keep a single expression on his face, one that maybe he thinks will be comforting to everyone in the room, including me. He's trying to look strong, army strong, "stop bleeding and keep marching" strong, but as Uncle Patrick wheels him forward, his face crumples and he puts up too much of a fight with his tears.

I want to jump out of the bed and run to him, to both him and Mom. I want to wrap my arms all the way around them and never let go again. But like my dad's leg, I am now cumbersome, heavy.

Uncle Patrick pushes Dad's wheelchair as close to my bed as possible. Mom slowly rises from hers, puts her hospital sock–covered feet on the ground, and begins walking towards me. Aunt Leslie holds her hands out behind Mom's back, as if to catch her should she fall.

Mom stops next to Dad. She gently rubs her palm against the top of his head, something she did more often when he used to shave his entire head bald, before he started letting it grow an inch or so.

"You shouldn't be on your feet," Dad says.

"No, you shouldn't be on *your* feet," she says and smiles. Her voice sounds hoarse, probably from all the screaming in the car. And maybe even more screaming after that. After learning about Isabelle.

"Oh, I get it," Dad says, looking down at his cast.

Maybe these were their first words to each other since the crash, since even before giving each other the silent treatment in the car. But that couldn't be. They must have talked about Isabelle. I wonder if they also think I'm Isabelle.

Every now and then Isabelle and I would trick our parents for fun. At church or at a party, we'd go into the bathroom and change our clothes, everything down to our shoes and the scrunchies in our hair.

We'd giggle endlessly while doing this, even as Isabelle was making fun of my body odor. I wonder if our parents, or anybody else, knew that our bodies had different smells.

Isabelle most often smelled like ginger and sometimes like the beach. No matter how hard I tried to fight it and wash it away, every now and then I would smell like sour milk. After we'd changed into each other's clothes, we'd wait for our parents to figure out what we had done. They never did.

We never went as far as sitting in on each other's classes, or taking each other's tests, but people thought we did anyway.

Two years ago, we punished a boy. His name was Joseph and he was the church youth choir director's nephew. He lived in Guadeloupe, where he was some kind of track star and was in their equivalent of junior year of high school. He'd come to Miami for a few months to learn English.

Isabelle and I would see him at choir rehearsal every Saturday, and he'd sing with the choir on Sundays. He was actually a decent singer, a good baritone. He thought he was being slick and asked us both out.

One Saturday evening, after choir rehearsal, we followed him down the church hallway and cursed him out in stereo. He was so shocked he never spoke to either of us again.

After that night, Isabelle and I made a pact. We would never let a guy come between us.

She made me pinkie swear.

"Sisters before dudes," she said.

I wonder if Joseph has heard about what happened. Is he now mourning Isabelle? I mean me.

This would be a good time to tell my parents about Isabelle and me having sometimes switched places to mess with them just a little. This is when I could say, I'm not playing now. This is for real. I'm not Isabelle. I'm Giselle.

Then, just as I am thinking this, I hear Mom shriek. She's breathing real hard and trying to get the words out.

"We made a mistake. A terrible mistake," she says.

"What is it?" Aunt Leslie asks her.

"Calm down, Sylvie," Dad says.

Mom leans over the bed railing. Her face is so close to mine that I can feel the warm spittle from her mouth spraying down on my face. Aunt Leslie and Alejandra try to pull her back so she can stop pressing her rib cage against the bed's railing.

"That's not Izzie!" Mom is shouting now. "This is not Isabelle. It's Giselle."

"What do you mean?" Dad shouts back.

Dad motions for Uncle Patrick to push his wheelchair even closer to where my head is. He takes me in, the swollen face and the body that won't move.

I imagine myself nodding, encouraging him, encouraging all of them to see me. I try to make my unmoving body stir, to show them a sign. I pretend that I can smile, even though I know my mouth isn't moving. I move my eyelids quickly, blink as much as possible.

Mom takes a few steps backwards and slides into her wheelchair.

"What are you saying?" Uncle Patrick asks her.

He, too, is trying to get a better look at my face.

"That's Giselle," Mom says without looking up.

"How can you be sure?" Aunt Leslie asks.

"How can you not be?" Mom says.

That's right, I want to say. You go, Mom! How could they not know who I am?

"Dave?" Uncle Patrick asks, seeking a second opinion from Dad.

"It's Giz," Dad says.

"You think?" Mom says, her sarcasm, which Isabelle inherited more than I, thankfully still intact.

"How do you tell them apart?" Aunt Leslie asks.

I never thought Aunt Leslie had trouble telling us apart. Either she'd been very good at faking it or we had always given her great clues.

"The little line from the stitches on her forehead," Mom says. "From that fall down the stairs at school."

"I don't see it," Dad says.

"How can you not see it?" Mom says. "Of course, you've been spending so little time at home. How would you even know?"

Are Mom and Dad now turning back into the couple they have been the past few weeks, the one whose every habit bothered the other, the one who's separating?

"We have to ask them to change the records," Mom says. "This is Giselle, not Isabelle."

"It's Giselle," Dad says, now sounding sure. Still, his whole body recoils. He begins coughing, loudly, painfully, the way Mom was coughing in the car during the crash, and when he stops coughing, he says, "They each have a black dot behind their ears, but on opposite sides. Look behind her ear and it's probably going to be on the right side."

If this was a different kind of situation, one in which people were allowed to laugh, I would have asked for a drumroll. But we don't need a drumroll. Both my parents are looking down at the floor as Aunt Leslie flicks my right ear.

My little bitty dot of a birthmark. Why would they even need to remember it? Mine is behind my right ear and Isabelle's is behind her left ear. It's one of the few ways our bodies are different. The other way I would have counted on, the different clothes we'd been wearing, had all been removed, erased by the crash. But this, my dot, thankfully was left.

Alejandra moves closer to have a better look. While our faces are nearly touching, she winks at me like she wants me to know that she's sure I'm in there, whoever I am.

"This is definitely *La Gemelita Número Dos*, Gemelita Giz."

Alejandra liked to call Isabelle and me *Las Gemelitas*. Isabelle was *La Gemelita Número Uno*, Gemelita Iz, and I was *La Gemelita Número Dos*, Gemelita Giz. We loved the sound of the words *gemelitas* or *mellizas*, which she also sometimes called us.

At least now they know who I am.

I feel like I've been stranded on a desert island and someone has finally found me.

"We have to change the records," Aunt Leslie says.

All the shouting must have drawn some attention. Finally a redheaded nurse arrives.

"I'm afraid everyone needs a rest," she says.

Aunt Leslie and Uncle Patrick push my parents' chairs as close to my bed as possible. While both Mom and Dad are looking at me, I know that they're feeling guilty for having mixed up Isabelle and me at such a crucial time. I know, too, that they want to hold me, just like I want to hold them. I know they want to tell me that everything is going to be all right, that we're now past the moment when we might have joined Isabelle.

Still, there's so much more I want to know. I want them to tell me exactly when Isabelle died. Will there be a funeral? Will I be able to go?

"I want to give her a kiss," Mom says.

The redheaded nurse lowers the bed's railing, and both Uncle Patrick and Aunt Leslie raise Mom from the wheelchair and carry her, it seems, all the way up to my face.

Mom's lips—wet, soft—feel hot against my skin, and that heat spreads throughout the rest of my body. Aunt Leslie and Uncle Patrick then help Mom back into her wheelchair, where she and Dad find themselves side by side. They reach out for each other's good hands and hold on tight. They must know now that being mad at each other makes no sense. Who else in the world can understand better what the other one is feeling?

Before Aunt Leslie and Uncle Patrick wheel them away, Dad lets go of Mom and blows me a kiss. "Goodbye, Giselle," he says. "We will see you soon."

How soon? I wonder. Tomorrow? The day after? The day after that?

CHAPTER 9

ISABELLE AND I used to try to imagine what our parents' days, especially school days, must have been like in Haiti.

Our vision of our parents' past is not totally made up. They had written each other letters when they were students in their first year of high school in Haiti's capital, Port-au-Prince. In the pictures from that time, Mom looks like a fourteen-year-old nun in her long navy skirt and white long-sleeved blouse. In his pictures, Dad is a beanpole, with a hint of a mustache.

Dad sat next to Mom in class, the year they started writing each other letters. In that class, the students were graded and ranked each week. Mom and Dad always took turns at being second and first.

One day Dad wrote Mom a letter saying, *I can no longer compete with you because I love you.*

Don't try to distract me, Mom wrote back. *My head won't be turned so easily. I will not be fooled by your tricks.*

Dad: *It's no trick. I love you.*

Mom: *What do you know about love? You're only a boy.*

Dad: *I didn't know much about love before, but I do now. Whether you accept it or not, you're teaching me both the sweetness and pain of love.*

"So corny." Isabelle kept rolling her eyes while we read parts of the letters out loud.

"Beyond corny," I agreed, even though we both found these younger versions of our parents too cute for words.

Dad fell behind in his studies.

It's your fault. He wrote a bunch of letters to Mom repeating the same thing. *I spend so much time thinking about you that I can't eat. I can't sleep. I can't study. I can't live without you.*

"I can't believe she fell for that stuff," Isabelle said. Though we might have easily fallen for something like it ourselves.

I notice you're losing weight, Mom wrote to follow through. *You're skin and bones already. You can't afford to lose any more weight. Let it not be said that I not only caused you to be kicked out of school, but caused you to die of starvation as well. I will be your girlfriend.*

Mom has all those letters in a box on the floor of their bedroom closet. Isabelle and I found them one day when Mom sent us to look for an old picture of Dad to turn into an invitation card for his fortieth birthday party.

Every now and then, when she and Dad aren't home, Isabelle and I look through those letters and use our French to decode them.

I let this story of the way our parents fell in love sink under with me.

I can almost feel the pieces of lined notebook paper they wrote their letters on in my hands. Some of the pages still have dried and flattened begonias glued to them.

Dad's letters, the ones with the flowers, are written in red ink in a firm handwriting that looks as though it had been practiced against a ruler. Mom's words are large and disorderly, as if to show that she couldn't care less.

CHAPTER 10

"SO, WE'VE BEEN calling you by the wrong name," the head neurologist, duck doctor, says in a combo newscaster and game show host voice when he comes through with his line of student duckling interns. Unlike the ducklings, he doesn't wear scrubs. He's super well dressed under his white coat, all classic, textured pastel shirts and slim, bold-colored silk ties. From my slanted perspective, though, he still seems to be shaped like a duck, a dabbler, with his head always tipped in one direction or another, but never lined up in the middle.

As he looks over my chart on his iPad, the head duck doctor starts telling interesting twin stories to the duckling interns.

There was the woman who gave birth to one black twin and one white one.

"Can anyone guess what the odds are of this happening even if both parents are biracial?" he asks the duckling interns while shining a light in my eyes for the umpteenth time.

I want to raise my hand—if only my hand still worked—to offer a guess.

Umm, let me see. A million to one.

It's always safe to go with a million to one for things like this.

The odds of anything really unusual happening is always a million to one. The odds of my family heading out to a concert one night and ending up three broken and one dead are probably somewhere near a million to one. The odds of Isabelle dying and the rest of us being alive are probably a million to one, too.

The head duck has now moved on to stories of twins raised apart, across the country, across the world, twins who end up basically living the same life, choosing the same profession, marrying the same kind of person, and having the same number of children, and giving them the same names. The separated twins in the duck doctor's stories sometimes run into each other accidentally at an amusement park, or sometimes in a hospital ward, where they're being treated for the same disease. Most of the time, they don't even realize there's a carbon copy of them out there until they come face-to-face.

He then moves on to conjoined twins.

"I've never had the pleasure of treating conjoined twins," he says. "What would be the likelihood of them walking into this hospital one day and needing our services?"

Oh me, me, me, I want to scream. Please pick me.

A million to one! A million to one is the likelihood of conjoined twins walking into this hospital and taking over the bed I'm in right now. Or would they need two beds?

"We know that craniopagus twins share a brain, but do they also share a mind?" the head duck asks.

That particular question is above everyone's pay grade, including mine, so the head duck tackles it himself.

"Some believe that identical twins share a single soul, so why wouldn't sharing a mind be possible for conjoined twins?"

"You mean the ones who share sensory input and impressions, where you prick one and the other cries?" a female duckling asks.

"Indeed," the head duck says. "Now, let's get back to this patient."

Soon after that, I tune out the head duck because he's offering less and less information I can use. I start paying attention again when he says this: "Don't be so shy, young lady. We're all eager to say hello. Old friends as well as new friends like me. You have nothing that a young brain like yours can't shake off."

I know what he's not saying. My sister took the brunt of it for me, for all of us. So I might as well do my part. I might as well get on with it. I might as well just snap out of it and wake up.

I want to wake up, but I can't. Because waking up might mean leaving Isabelle behind forever.

When the head duck and the ducklings walk out, I'm happy to have some relief from the heat of the flashlight on my pupils, but also the heat of the head duck's breath on my face. I could tell, for one thing, that he'd just had breakfast. Something sweet, strawberries. Maybe I'm smelling strawberries now after these twins stories because Isabelle loved strawberries. She loved strawberries like I loved Jean Michel Brun.

In the classroom I imagine myself in that afternoon, Jean Michel Brun is sitting where he always is, between me and my best friend, Tina. He's doing something he often does, drawing us, or alternate versions of us.

That afternoon, he draws us in tutus, like ballerinas.

He passes me a note again.

DO YOU WANT TO MEET LATER?

This time I write back.

Tina's house?

Cool, he scribbles at the bottom of the paper.

Jean Michel, Tina, and I became a trio when we were actually grouped together for an assignment for Mr. Rhys's class.

Tina is Pastor Ben's granddaughter. She and I have known each other our whole lives. She is the person I take all the same classes with and wear the same kind of clothes with. If Isabelle wasn't in the same school, people might have called Tina my twin.

When Tina, Isabelle, and I were together, Tina was just as likely to finish my sentences as Isabelle was.

Tina and her parents were supposed to meet us at the spring orchestra concert the evening of the crash. We'd agreed that whoever got there first would save seats for the others. Jean Michel was coming to the concert, too, and Tina and I were going to watch out for him.

Before we left the house, Tina and I had spoken on the phone. I had a cell phone. Where is my cell phone now? Where's Isabelle's cell phone? Our phones were in Mom's purse during the car ride.

Mom made us give her our phones before we pulled away from the house. She didn't want us to spend the whole car ride texting. She'd give them back to us after the concert, she said.

"I'll see you soon," I'd told Tina on the cell phone before we left the house.

"Soon," she'd said.

I wonder if Tina has come to see me in the hospital. I wonder if Jean Michel has been at my bedside without me realizing it.

DO YOU WANT TO MEET LATER?

Tina's house!

Jean Michel, Tina, and I met at Tina's house for our assignment for Mr. Rhys's class. They were also working on another assignment for their computer science lab. Even though both Jean Michel and Tina were practically Internet geniuses, Mr. Rhys still insisted that we use index cards for our group presentation.

When I arrived, the rainbow pack index cards were lined up on Tina's dining room table next to Jean Michel's and Tina's laptops. Our presentation was going to be on Jean Michel's namesake, Jean-Michel Basquiat.

I tried to keep my eyes off Jean Michel Brun's face as we worked, leaning in real close to copy facts off his laptop.

Did we know that Jean-Michel Basquiat threw a pie in his high school principal's face? our Jean Michel asked.

Tina already knew this, but she couldn't stop laughing. Tina's laughter is so loud that it's traveling through time and filling up my hospital room. I think I feel Tina's always cold hands on top of mine in the hospital room and I see her egg-shaped face leaning down close to mine and I hear her full-of-bells voice telling me something I can't quite grasp. I think I see Jean Michel, too. I see both of them standing on opposite sides of my hospital bed, trying to help me remember that afternoon at Tina's house.

Then I feel Jean Michel's lips brush against mine, right there in the hospital room. He's trying to breathe words and pictures into my mouth. My body registers this as not just a jolt, but as a long, slow-motion glide down a waterslide, with Jean Michel right behind me, on a school trip. Or as his open palm grazing my shoulder while he walks to his seat in our classroom. Or those Narcissus-level stares.

Jean Michel's lips rest on top of mine for a few seconds, and I do my best to raise my head so the kiss can last longer. So he and I can last longer. But I remain the other Sleeping Beauty, the one who will not be awakened by a kiss.

"I can't even imagine being so famous," Jean Michel said that afternoon at Tina's house. That's when I heard his slight stutter for the first time.

"Obviously your parents could imagine it," Tina said. "They named you after the other Jean-Michel."

"My mom was my age when he died from that drug over-dose," our Jean Michel said. "She was kind of in love with him."

Tina bowed her head in deference, as though she wanted to call for a moment of silence for Basquiat's drug overdose. But then she quickly perked up and added, "If you can't imagine being that famous, then you'll never be."

"That's the preacher's granddaughter speaking," I said. "Tina's heard too many sermons."

"None that you haven't heard," Tina said.

"You guys go to church?" Jean Michel asked.

"Almost every Sunday," Tina said.

"I'd like to come sometime," he said. Then I saw him staring at me long and hard for once. He was looking at me like I was the church, the pew, the choir, all of it. He was looking at me like he would be coming to me.

Tina cleared her throat, then coughed. Jean Michel smiled and looked away.

"We love having folks at church," Tina said, sounding for a moment like her grandfather recruiting from his pulpit.

After Jean Michel left, Tina raised her hand to her forehead and fake swooned.

"There goes Jean Michel Brun," she said. "The great and eternal love of your life."

CHAPTER 11

MOM COMES BACK to see me the next day.

She's alone, without Dad or Aunt Leslie or Uncle Patrick. From the time she's wheeled through the front door by a super hunky male nurse, she never stops talking.

"You can come back for me later," she tells him, waving him off. "I'm going to be here a while."

He wheels her as close to my IV pole as possible, then he walks away.

Mom looks calmer than the last time I saw her, after she realized that I wasn't Isabelle. Even the bandages across her forehead seem less strange to me now, as though they have become a normal part of her.

"Leslie had to go back to Orlando for the day," she says, "to see about one of her critical patients. Seems like we're not the only critical patients in the world."

Yes! Her sarcasm is in full force, what Dad calls her ironic humor. This means that she's holding up well. She's getting stronger.

"I told Patrick and Alejandra to go back to the house and get some rest," she says. "Soon everyone will have to go back to their lives and it will be just you, me, and Dad."

Where's Dad, I wonder. Why hadn't he come, too?

"Dad's in surgery," she says, her voice rising with real-sounding cheerfulness. She puts both her hands in her lap, tugging at her hospital gown now and then.

Dad, in surgery?

From the chair, she can see my face. She can see all of me, which I imagine is nothing cheerful, though perhaps it might be a bit more hopeful than the alternative. I am alive, after all.

I imagine, too, that she can read my face, even though it's impossible for me to move any part of it, impossible for me to speak, to ask questions.

So she's sitting there and trying to *read me*. That's the only way we can have a conversation now. She'll have to sit there and try to read my mind.

"Something was off in your dad's arm," she says. "They had to go back and reset the bone."

She pauses as if waiting for me to react, as if waiting for me to raise my voice and respond.

Poor Dad.

"Poor David," she says. "He's lucky he didn't break more bones."

Lucky, lucky. Everyone is so lucky. Everyone except Isabelle.

"*Lucky* may not be the right word, uh?" she says.

So it's working. She is reading me, understanding me, like Isabelle might if she was sitting there.

"Dad will be okay," she says.

I can tell that she's doing her best not to bring up Isabelle. But how can she not bring up Isabelle? Every day from now on will be a day without Isabelle, every ordinary day, as well as every special day.

"My ribs were bruised, but they're going to heal," she says. "They tell me I might be able to go home tomorrow. There are no casts for ribs."

No casts indeed. But I am starting to understand that some internal injuries are worse than the ones you can actually see.

"Soon we'll all, well, the three of us will be able to go home," she says.

Does that mean that she and Dad would now stay together? Has something that was meant to kill us, something that's killed Isabelle, reunited them? Has the crash brought them back together?

I never quite understood why they were separating in the first place. Everything seemed fine until it wasn't. They'd been like any other parents, snapping at each other now and then, but then making up soon afterwards. The giggles had grown less frequent, the arguments more so, in hushed tones, along with Dad's pleas for understanding, Mom's sobs.

Even with all of that, the separation announcement had seemed unnecessarily drastic and sudden. Like the crash.

You wake up on a sunny day and go to school. You come back home and have dinner. You get in a car and nothing is ever the same again. Everything changes.

Some things are just unstoppable. You have no control over them. My parents' separation had grown to seem that way. And now there's nowhere to go but back. Like the stories that keep popping up in my mind, stories from the life I had before, about the way things used to be.

So it makes sense that Mom and Dad want to go back, too. Back to a place where everything seemed okay. Back to when Isabelle was alive. Back to when we were all together.

"I know a policewoman came to see you," she says, changing the subject. "An officer, a detective."

Yes, the policewoman.

I want to hear all about the policewoman. What did the policewoman mean when she said that what happened might not have been an accident? Maybe Mom knows.

Mom pulls herself up by grabbing the sides of the wheelchair. Her face tightens and she is beginning to sweat. Sweat rolls down her cheeks from underneath the bandage on her forehead. She looks like she's in a lot of pain, but soon she's standing without help. She takes a cup and straw from the side table, then pushes the straw past my lips.

I try to press the top of my mouth down on the straw to pull the water up, but I can't get more than one drop. Mom moves my face to the side so that one drop of water will slide out and not choke me. That drop of water tastes really good. I had been craving it without realizing it. I wish there were ice cubes for her to rub against my lips the way the nurses do.

Looking defeated, she pulls the straw out, then takes a few sips herself. After she puts the foam cup down, she's shaking so much that it looks like she's going to fall down. She holds on to the bed's railing to balance herself.

Sit down! I want to scream. Sit down now!

She looks back at the wheelchair as though she's carefully measuring the distance, the one or two steps she'd have to walk to get back to it. She grunts as she takes those steps, backwards, then she plops herself down quickly into the chair.

"Ouchie," she says.

Isabelle liked to say, "Ouchie." Never *ouch*, but *ouchie*. We all started saying *ouchie* because of her.

"Let me rest a minute," Mom says, catching her breath.

After she's rested a bit, she says, "The funny thing is that the girl who hit us is fine. She's not even in jail. She's out. She's fine and Isabelle is gone."

Who is this girl, I wonder. What kind of person would drive that way? And kill a person and be fine?

The hunky male nurse—I realize now that he has a beard—walks back into the room. He looks down disapprovingly at Mom, as though he can tell that she's been doing something she's not supposed to.

"Your husband's out of surgery and he's asking for you," he says.

Mom looks relieved. I can tell that everything is now a big deal. Little things now mean a whole lot. You can die going to a concert, so why can't you die in surgery? Or from just lying in a hospital bed? Why can't you die from broken ribs for which there are no casts?

Mom raises her hands and waves goodbye as the nurse wheels her out. And I know now that for the rest of our lives there will be no simple goodbyes.

Mom is a woman of style, a stylish woman, some might say. She can wear the heck out of a hat, especially a black one. She knows how to walk in really high heels without seeming like she's walking on stilts. She always knows all the best lipstick–eye shadow combos. She knows how to make a great flower arrangement for any party, even without flowers. At home, her desk is the definition of neatness. Before the crash, short, twisted plaits draped where her bandages are now.

Sometimes she'd wear her sunglasses inside the house, like a movie star. Her jewelry is always simple but elegant: diamond stud earrings, her spaghetti-thin platinum wedding ring, and a gold Tiffany bracelet Dad bought her for one of their wedding anniversaries. Her "core" is usually toned to the hilt, and whether her weight goes up or down, she always wears her bikini to the beach to show off the small wreath of red and yellow begonias tattooed in a circle around her belly button and in the middle of her back. Her tattoo seems to have entered on one side of her body and burst out of the other. Like a bullet. At times it also looks like it has roots, growing into her abdomen and spine. Mom accidently pressed the inside of her left elbow against a charcoal grill when she was Isabelle's and my age. That scar now looks like a sepia picture of a russet forest. When her body fights, it wins.

When Isabelle and I were little, before Mom would leave us alone in a room or walk a few inches behind us on a narrow sidewalk, she'd always lean over and whisper to both of us that we should just holler, "Rele, *if you need me.*"

Somehow, even as little girls, we knew that this was a promise she would always keep. Wherever we were, we knew that the slightest whimper would bring her to our side. She'd proven it to us many times, at the first sound of a wail, a scream. When we felt water rushing into our noses in a pool. When our tricycles rolled too fast ahead of her, when we scraped a knee or elbow on a pebble or a rock. She'd swoop out of nowhere and rescue us.

The hunky bearded male nurse doesn't know any of this. The doctors don't know it, either. And maybe Dad has forgotten, too. I certainly had.

After Mom leaves, I hear the faint sound of the radio again. This time there's music playing. A faint flute solo. I try to move my head forward to hear it better, but my head is going nowhere.

I imagine Isabelle raising the flute to her lips and swaying her upper body in a half circle, the way she sometimes did when trying a piece out on me. I close my eyes the way Isabelle often did when practicing without her sheet music.

Isabelle is now standing at my bedside, with both her hands, her perfect, unhurt hands, resting on the railing of my hospital bed. She's wearing her orchestra uniform, the white blouse, black pencil skirt, and black bow tie, the same one she was wearing in the car, the one she, Mom, and I had picked out together, out of five possible options, at the mall. Her braids are brushed up and piled on top of her head, with a few strands left hanging to frame her unbruised face. Around her neck is the gold chain, the Hand of Fatima, that Aunt Leslie had given us.

In the dream, I can speak, so I tell her, "Hi."

"Hi yourself," she answers.

"Remember that time you asked me to trim your eyebrows and I plain shaved them off so you wouldn't look so much like me? I'm sorry about that," I say.

"I had no business trying to trim my eyebrows," she says. "I was twelve. I'm sorry I asked you to undress in the middle of the street that time you were wearing my Emeline T-shirt."

"Thank God I was wearing a bra," I say.

"One of your better ones," she says.

"Actually it was yours, too," I say.

Then, her voice sounding both bubbly and nervous, she says, "You stun me. You astonish me."

I know she's borrowing "astonish" from *Little Women*. But the "stun me" is all hers. She liked to say "Stun me" the way other people say "Bite me." It was also her way of saying "Impress me." So if you told her you could walk ten miles, she might say, "Stun me and walk twenty."

"You've really astonished me here," she says, looking down at me in the bed. "You've been great. Super great. For the rest of your life, you keep stunning me. Just keep stunning me."

"Are you here to say goodbye?" I ask her.

"We'll never say goodbye," she says.

I remember learning in my seventh-grade science class how sounds might possibly live on forever. We were doing a lesson on Guglielmo Marconi, the inventor of the radio. Guglielmo

Marconi thought that one day a machine would be invented that would pick up sounds that had been floating in the air since the beginning of time. He believed that sometime in the future we'd all be able to hear the original cave dwellers moan, Jesus weep, Leonardo da Vinci lecture, or our own first cries as babies.

I would always hear the sound of the crash, the clang of metal against glass. I would always hear Isabelle's voice shouting, "We're late! We're late!"

"I'm so sorry for everything I've ever done to you," I tell her.

"No worries," she says, just as she always did after we fought. And she would mean it, too. There would be no grudge after that.

"No worries at all, Gizzie." She stops to listen to the radio sonata, turning her face towards the door as if to see where the music is coming from.

"You're not going to die," she says, her face tilted towards the music.

"You're not going to live," I say.

"I could have told you that," she says, smiling.

"I wish I'd known," I say.

I want to cry, but I can't. It is as if crying is forbidden in that type of dream. So instead I say, "I love you."

"I love you, too," she says.

I don't remember us ever saying "I love you" to each other before. We never needed to.

"I love you," I say again, wishing I could say it for every other time that I could have said it in the past. Before I can say it again, the music stops and she's gone.

We had been fighting in the car.

Before she asked Dad to put the CD in, we had been fighting. She kept saying. "We're late" or "We're going to be late" and I was tired of it. I was tired of hearing her voice, when I just wanted to sit there and think about Jean Michel Brun. I wanted to look pretty for him, and I wasn't sure I was looking pretty enough. I would have liked one more chance to change my clothes again. Another fifteen minutes to pick another outfit, to touch up my makeup. So when she said, "We're going to be late" for the hundredth time, I shouted at her. I yelled, "Chill!"

And she calmly answered, "You're the one who needs to chill."

"What's wrong with you?" she asked.

"What's wrong with you?" I yelled.

"*Les filles!*" Mom shouted.

"What's wrong with both of you?" Dad turned his head and gave us a long, harsh stare from the front seat. Maybe too long a stare.

"You're not some famous rock star," I continued. "You're just going to play in a stupid high school orchestra."

That seemed to finally get her, but she didn't want to show it. Instead she opened the flute case—a flute case I'd helped her pick out—pulled out the practice CD, and handed it to Dad. She wanted to help me chill. She wanted us all to chill. She also wanted me to see that this stupid high school orchestra was important to her.

"Let's hear this how the 'Maestro' intended it before we butcher it," she said. She was trying to rise above, act more mature than me.

Relieved, Dad turned around again to take the CD from her. Maybe he looked away from the wheel for too long.

Then *The Firebird*.

Then the oncoming red minivan.

Then the crash.

I wish that rather than shouting at her, I had simply said, "Yes, we're late." That way she wouldn't have had to shout back at me, and Dad wouldn't have had to get excited, and maybe a little bit less attentive at the wheel.

Details, funny how they are the first to go.

In a long line of fuzzy events, we lose the details first.

CHAPTER 12

THEY SAY AFTER people have been together for a long time, they start to look alike. My parents are not there yet, but my dad's parents, Grandpa Marcus and Grandma Régine, look like they could be twins, frats, fraternals. Old age has even shrunken them down to the same height. Grandpa Marcus used to hover around six feet two, but now he's about five seven like Grandma Régine. They have the same roundness about them, too.

"From eating the same meals all the time and getting about the same amount of no exercise," they always say. They speak like a duet. Even their silence is in stereo.

Having come all the way from Haiti, they spend hours at the hospital, starting that afternoon. They take turns going across the hospital walkway between my room and Mom's and Dad's.

When they are with me, they don't ask my doctors and nurses questions. They don't give me updates, either. They just sit there staring at me or reading a book.

When the nurses walk in, they don't wait to be asked to leave, they simply walk out, one behind the other. When they come back, the one who left the room last is the first one through the door. They wear the same types of beige-shaded outfits, too, but in different combinations. Sometimes I see the same black fedora or panama hat on each of their salt-and-pepper hair at different times of the day. Same goes for Grandpa Marcus's linen jackets, which he is rarely without.

Grandma Régine does most of the silent reading, occasionally passing her book to Grandpa Marcus, who, ever the architect, might spend up to fifteen minutes, when he's not drawing or looking at drawings, studying a passage that Grandma Régine has casually pointed out to him. Sometimes he'll go way beyond the lines she's showing him and only return the book when she nudges him.

Every once in a while, Grandpa Marcus will get up, pat his jacket pocket, then walk out of the room. When he returns, he smells of cigarettes. Grandma Régine wriggles her nose as if to confirm what she smells. Then she keeps reading.

I want so badly to beg her to read to me. Read to me, I want to tell her. I would love to hear your voice.

Grandma Régine never liked the sound of her voice. It was

always more gruff than her personality, which was already a bit grumpy to begin with. Someone must have told her along the way that she didn't have a nice voice, so she stopped using her voice as much as she should. She never read to Isabelle and me when she watched us when we were little. She would just hand us books and the three of us would read quietly, separately.

Grandpa Marcus's specialty is not as a reading companion, though, but as a jokester. He loves to tell odd little stories, which would put my parents and their Haitian friends in stitches, but which Isabelle and I never found funny. I remember one joke that was related to his not-so-secret on-and-off smoking.

A man who is about to be executed is offered a final cigarette. He turns it down because it is bad for his health. All of Grandpa Marcus's jokes are like that. Unfunny in the worst way. But he just laughs and laughs at them, even if no one else does.

I wish Grandpa Marcus would tell me one of those jokes now, but this is not a place for jokes. It's a place for people appearing and disappearing. Both in my dreams and in person.

While Grandma Régine and Grandpa Marcus are sitting there, I feel like I'm back with them and Isabelle way up in the hills above Port-au-Prince.

The sky is cornflower blue over their estate, their Victorian-inspired house and their boundless-looking garden, which overlooks the city below. In the middle of the garden is a two-hundred-year-old silk-cotton tree. Like the house, the silk-cotton tree is still standing in spite of a massive earthquake that nearly destroyed the city a few years back.

At over two hundred and fifty feet tall, the silk-cotton tree is the tallest tree that Isabelle and I have ever seen. It is so high that when we were little we thought it would take a whole week to climb it. It's so wide that both Isabelle and I could hug it and not touch hands in the middle. Parts of the trunk, where we once carved our names, have ridges so deep that both our bodies could fit into them. Sometimes, at night, especially when there was thunder or lightning, the silk-cotton tree would light up, too, with fireflies. During the day, the roots stretched out over the ground, like snakes slithering away from their nests.

The day before we left Grandma Régine and Grandpa Marcus's house last summer, Isabelle and I spotted something that we'd often noticed while sitting on their terrace. It was raining somewhere beyond the harbor, above the sea, and around the cloud-shrouded sun was a kind of halo, a circular rainbow that Grandpa Marcus called a *gloire*, a "glory."

Every time we'd see a glory, Isabelle and I would keep our eyes on it until the rain would stop and it would start to fade.

We would then close our eyes and imagine that it was still there, even after it was long gone.

"We won't say a full goodbye to it," Isabelle would say. "We're each going to say half."

Then she would say "Good" and I would say "Bye" right before we'd reopen our eyes to a glory-less world.

The best part of having a birthday party for two is the invitations. Mom always insisted that Isabelle and I make all our invitations. Over the years, we've made birthday party invitations shaped like flowers, balloons, cowboy boots, and movie theater tickets. We've even passed out invitations inside recycled plastic bottles.

Our birthday parties have mostly been at our house. But Mom and Dad have also rented out jungle gyms, ballet studios, restaurants, and hotel rooms. And of course there was the Disney party and the early birthday trip to Mexico that Aunt Leslie had organized.

Our last birthday party was a girls-only sleepover in a downtown Miami hotel room with Tina and a few girls from church, Lois and some other girls from orchestra and debate team— Isabelle's freshman- and sophomore-year obsession. We ate pizza in our pajamas and tried to watch a bunch of sappy romantic comedies that we didn't see the end of because we were talking so much.

Isabelle and I were going to spend our next birthday with the entire family at Grandpa Marcus and Grandma Régine's house in Haiti. Tina was even supposed to come.

Our seventeenth birthday party invitation was going to be in the shape of a glory. This would have been one of our best birthdays yet.

CHAPTER 13

I AM NOW deaf. I imagine Isabelle trying to comfort me by telling me that Beethoven went deaf, too.

Everything is quiet. Total and absolute quiet. The duck doctor and his ducklings come and shine the penlight into my eyes and poke at the bottom of my feet, but I can't hear what they're saying.

I can't hear the few words Grandpa Marcus and Grandma Régine whisper to each other in my presence. I feel like I'm in a soundproof cage. The world is a silent movie, playing out in 3-D around me.

My freshman year at Morrison, I took an art class where the teacher, Ms. Walker, taught us origami. We were supposed to fold our handmade washi paper into whatever shapes we wanted. I wanted to make silence.

I looked up the Japanese letters for *silence*, which vaguely looked like two figures dancing. And when I finally managed to fold the paper into those shapes, everyone in the class, including Ms. Walker, thought that I had made Isabelle and me.

I miss the faint sound of the radio at night.

I miss music.

Even though Isabelle used to say I was tone-deaf, I miss my tone deafness. I miss echoes, the sounds of footsteps, and the nurses tiptoeing in and out in the middle of the night. I miss the intercom announcements, telling the staff about lunchtime seminars and Zumba classes. I miss all the other announcements urging the doctors and nurses to report to patients' rooms or to the nurses' station. I miss the sounds of shift changes, distant sirens, and car horns.

Now, the only voices I hear are in my head.

In the total silence of the hospital room, I try not to think too much about Isabelle. Because if she comes to me now, if I keep dreaming about her, I will never wake up. I will never leave here.

Instead, I think about Jean Michel Brun.

DO YOU WANT TO MEET UP LATER? He passed me a note in class when we came back to school after New Year's.

While Isabelle and I were in New York at Uncle Patrick's apartment that New Year's Eve of the blizzard, Jean Michel Brun called me on my cell phone as we were watching the Times

Square ball drop on television. Isabelle and I had begged Uncle Patrick to take us to some exciting music industry party, but we had worn him out that day and he was too exhausted to leave the house. Besides, he never went out on New Year's Eve, Uncle Patrick said. He liked to stay in and reflect.

He wasn't looking for a girlfriend or anything, Jean Michel told me. It sounded like he was reflecting, too. He had just broken up with someone who was going to another school, and he wasn't sure he was over her yet.

"You might have texted me all this or written me a long email," I said.

"Or I could have drawn you a picture," he said. "But I wanted to hear your voice."

"Why aren't you at a party or something?" I asked.

"Why aren't you?" he said.

"Happy New Year," I said as the ball landed.

This was going to be the best year of my life.

Until it wasn't.

Early in the new year, one day after school, Jean Michel and I went to a restaurant called Chez Moy in Little Haiti. The place was my idea. He had written, *Do you want to meet up later?* And I had written back, *Chez Moy*.

Chez Moy was surrounded by mechanics' shops, storefront churches, and record shops that blasted music from giant loud-speakers on the sidewalk. The owner of the restaurant, Moy, was one of Dad's old army buddies, whom he'd encouraged to move to Miami years ago. Moy was running for city commis-sioner in District 3, which includes Little Haiti. Pictures of him and his massive biceps, fully visible in his camouflage T-shirt, covered the restaurant walls.

Sitting across from Jean Michel, I nervously scratched at the roots of my braids while he tugged at his earring.

"I hear you want to go to art school," he said.

"Who told you that?" I asked.

Then we both blurted out at the same time, "Tina!"

So he'd been talking to Tina. In computer science lab. About me.

"I'd like to go to art school, too," he said.

Then we should go together, I wanted to say, but held back.

"I might try it on my own first, though," he said. "Like Basquiat."

"Basquiat was great," I said.

"So are we," he said.

I felt my cheeks flaming with embarrassment.

"That's why we got an A on that project," he added.

We were all still proud of that A, as though it was some masterpiece that the three of us had created together.

The waiter came and we ordered white rice and bean sauce, fried plantains—his plantains sweet, mine green. He spent a lot of time picking out the little islands of fat on his black bean sauce, making fork tracks in the plate of rice in front of him. I concentrated on my salad, fishing beneath the lettuce leaves as though someone had hidden a secret prize for me there. He had this habit of bopping his head as though a melody had just popped into it. I could almost see him doing that as he tried to think of something else to say.

He kept staring into his water glass, raising his face now and then to say something nice about the food, which he obviously hated.

Moy came out of the back room to say hello, and this seemed to impress Jean Michel. But Moy was really looking for volunteers to work in his campaign office.

If we volunteered, Moy said, we wouldn't have to pay for our meals.

Even though we didn't have to pay, Jean Michel left a ten-dollar tip for the waiter, which I like to think he did to impress me.

That weekend, Jean Michel and I went to Moy's campaign office to help with Moy's computer operations. We organized his call sheets and mailing lists by merging a bunch of databases.

"I have something for you," Jean Michel said when we were

done organizing Moy's personal files. We also found Moy a new list of potential donors, which made him so happy that he offered to adopt us, if we didn't like our parents.

What Jean Michel had for me was a framed postcard-size drawing of my face washed out with red and blue paint, in the style of Shepard Fairey. I was too flustered to speak, so I just leaned over and gave him a quick peck on the lips.

That was our first kiss.

At Moy's victory-night party, several hundred people packed themselves into the restaurant. As soon as Mom, Dad, Isabelle, and I walked in, Jean Michel motioned for me to meet him in the back terrace. We found an uncrowded corner and he wrapped his arms around my shoulders as we listened to the speeches and cheers coming from inside.

"I have something to confess," he whispered.

We were standing so close that he didn't have to whisper, but he did anyway.

"What is it?" I asked.

I tried to make my voice sound all breathy and sultry, but it only made it harder for him to understand me.

"I can't help but feel like I am the one who won tonight," he said.

A few nights later, my parents, Isabelle, and I met the Marshalls at this monthly outdoor concert called Big Night in Little Haiti. Tina's dad, Mr. Marshall, another old army buddy of Dad's, was an aviation specialist with the US Coast Guard and didn't get a lot of time off. He was there with us that night, and he and Dad were so happy to see each other that neither they nor our moms were watching us too closely.

The muraled plaza in front of the Little Haiti Cultural Center was packed with hundreds of people dancing and singing along with Emeline, the queen of Haitian music, and one of Isabelle's favorite singers.

I'd asked Jean Michel to meet me near the stage. Isabelle wandered off to find some of her friends, and Tina and I went off to find Jean Michel. We found him staring dreamily at Emeline, who was belting out a heartbreaker of a ballad. Emeline was looking her most beautiful that night. Her piercing eyes and signature alluring smile were in full effect. She wore her hair bare and closely cropped for some songs, and wrapped in exquisite head scarves for others. Her earrings were like miniature sculptures, and her head wraps and dresses were so intricately draped, layered, and embroidered that they could be hanging at the Smithsonian next to the gowns of first ladies and, well, other queens.

Jean Michel, Tina, and I stood under a canopy near the stage. We were mesmerized by Emeline's sultry yet mournful voice, as people slow danced or squashed their bodies together around us.

Afterwards, Isabelle somehow managed to get backstage

with one of her friends and, when Emeline wasn't looking, took one of her earrings from her dressing room and slipped it into her pocket. It was a long, shoulder-grazing chandelier earring made with tiny rainbow-colored butterflies. Isabelle never wore the earring, as I thought she would, but she stuffed it in one of the flute case's interior dividers, for luck.

The evening closed with a spirited procession, like a "second line" parade. The three of us joined the procession line bouncing behind Emeline, until we were too sweaty and tired to continue.

At some point I bent over and grabbed my knees to catch my breath and I felt Jean Michel's hand on my spine, and it was almost like I grew wings there. I felt lighter than I have ever felt in my whole life.

Our stares became a little more intense at school after that, but we didn't sneak off into corners, or skip classes to go to the movies, like I wanted to. We were waiting for that night, the night of the concert, to sit next to each other and let everybody know. I wanted to look so perfect for him that I took an extra fifteen minutes and made us late. Now, in the silent hospital room, Jean Michel's drawing of me, the one I had hanging next to a Basquiat print on my bedroom wall, is right next to my necklace in what is beginning to look like one of those roadside memorials. Something like that would probably be made for Isabelle near the crash site.

CHAPTER 14

WHEN MOM AND Dad and Aunt Leslie come to visit later that day, I still can't hear. They are all mimes now, beautiful mimes, in a strange play. Their stage is this small room with the glass bricks on the wall. Their props are the wheelchairs that Grandpa Marcus and Aunt Leslie are pushing them in. Grandma Régine is the understudy, who's not sure what to do with herself. She walks back and forth between the two wheelchairs to see if anyone needs anything.

What everyone needs she cannot provide. What everyone needs is to not be here, to be unhurt, to be with Isabelle.

Mom and Dad look a lot better. Dad's hurt leg is still stretched out in front of him, his arm folded into a cast. His face looks a lot less prickly, though, a lot less battered, as does Mom's.

Mom is wearing a pink knit cap that Grandma Régine must have bought her. I can imagine Grandma Régine just handing her the cap and saying, "This will cover your bandage." And not much more. She would never ask Mom if she wanted a cap or what color she'd like. That's just the way Grandma Régine is.

The cap looks good on Mom. It doesn't slip off or anything. When Mom pushes herself up by holding the sides of the wheelchair, she doesn't seem to be in as much pain as before. And when she bends down to kiss my forehead, it doesn't seem as agonizing as the first or second time. Her body sways back and forth a bit. Aunt Leslie mouths off a warning, then rushes over and helps Mom to back into her wheelchair.

Dad looks worried. He cringes along with Mom. Then both my parents are just sitting there looking at me. Occasionally they ask Aunt Leslie some questions that seem to be about me. Aunt Leslie's lips move carefully, as though she's trying to think of more doctorly answers.

I make up dialogue for them.

Mom: *How much longer do you think she'll be here?*

Aunt Leslie: *Time will tell. We just have to be patient.*

Dad: *You just made a doctor's pun.*

Mom: *But we're waiting for her to be part of Isabelle's funeral service. We want her to say goodbye.*

That last part I think Mom actually does say. If I read her lips correctly. But the rest, I am not so sure.

What they're actually saying is probably much more interesting. They might be talking about the weather, about Aunt Leslie's beautiful green dress. Mom is probably wishing that she was wearing it instead of her hospital gown.

They keep staring at me. I wish I could talk to them with my eyes. I wish I could speak to them the way I'd spoken to Isabelle in that dream. I wish I could tell them that I'd already said goodbye to Isabelle. In our own way. In the language of the palms.

I wish I could tell them not to worry so much about me, that I am in here somewhere and will eventually resurface. But how can I be sure that things aren't getting even worse? I want to make small talk, really small talk, like "Hi." Just "Hi" might be enough. I just want them to know that I'm still here, that I still know who they are. I want them to know that I still love them. But they all sit there and keep looking at me, as though they're holding a vigil.

I'm tired of my silence. I'm tired of having all these thoughts racing through my head. Even if I can't hear them, I want to be able to say something. Just "Hi," not much more. Just so they know that I'm trying so hard to come back.

So I begin with my toes. I try to think of how I can make my toes move. My toes would have to move first. It's where the doctor keeps poking me. If only I can get one of my pinkie toes to move.

I draw a sketch of it in my mind. I even sing it to the tune of "Frère Jacques." *Pinkie to-e. Pinkie to-e. Just move please. Just move please.* I try and I try and I try. And they all sit there looking at me. They can't see how hard I'm trying. I'm trying to do what my dad in his army speak might call "signaling." But I have no flares or smoke grenades. I know Morse code but can't use it.

The last science project I did for physics class was about parasitic drag, the energy it takes to move things through water or air. Airplanes have to deal with it, as do swimmers in the ocean. It's a lot harder to move forward than to fall back. I have to remind myself that no matter how hard it seems, I just can't keep falling back.

CHAPTER 15

SOMETIMES IN MY dreams, I walk down an empty hospital hallway. My legs are shaky and my knees buckle. I'm not sure where I'm going. All I know is that I have to get there.

Soon, other patients start to appear. They range from toddlers in their parents' arms, to first graders, to kids who look way too old to be under eighteen. Some are sitting up in bed. Others are dragging IV poles behind them while pacing around their rooms. They only look up for a moment as I walk by.

When I feel dizzy, I lean against the dark grey hallway walls and rest. But I know I must keep walking. I must find Isabelle.

I feel like the girl in the magic act, the one the magician splits in half. The top part is me—the head that is leaning against the wall as I catch my breath—the rest is Isabelle.

Ahead looms the nurses' station. The nurses say nothing to me as I walk by. They're looking at computer screens, typing fast. I keep walking down the hall until I reach a room that is just like mine, a small room with glass bricks on the walls. Inside, lying there in a bed identical to mine, I see Isabelle. She looks exactly like I do, the way she always has.

She waves me in from the doorway until I'm close enough to touch her.

"Izzie," I say.

"Hey," she says.

"Izzie, I'm sorry I made us late."

"No way," she says, gesturing as if to brush that thought away.

"Fifteen minutes earlier—"

"I was late, too," she says.

Then I remember her scurrying around the house, pulling her black skirt out of the dryer, then yanking white blouses off hangers and dumping the ones she wouldn't be wearing on the bathroom floor. She was putting on her makeup while talking on the phone, making plans for beyond that night, for some homework she'd have to catch up on, some essay she'd have to write.

At some point I heard her talking to Ron Johnson.

"Wow, Ron," she kept saying. "We'll have to try that again."

I felt jealous. Of Ron Johnson?

It sounded like she had been to his house and was planning to go there again. There was no time to ask her about that. We were both doing too many things at once. We were both terrified that the boys we liked wouldn't like us enough. We were both anxious about what might come next. We were both late.

I reach out and hold her hands the same way I remember holding them in the car. I think of how hard we tried not to let go when we thought we were both dying.

I stand there all night holding her hands.

The magician has not yet arrived with his box and his saw. We are not yet cut in half. We are still fully ourselves. We are still entwined. We are still whole.

In some versions of this dream, Mom and Dad travel down the hallway with me. Mom with her pink knit bonnet and Dad being pushed by Mom in his wheelchair.

Always when they arrive, it hits me again that I have to keep saying goodbye to Isabelle.

Never in my wildest dreams would I ever think that we'd all be there now, in this room, saying goodbye to Isabelle. Which goes to show you that Aunt Leslie was wrong. Isabelle and I don't have any special powers. If we did, I would have seen this coming. And if I knew all this was coming, I wouldn't have spent so much time getting dressed to impress Jean Michel that night. I wouldn't have taken so much time changing seven or eight times. I wouldn't have forgotten my cell phone on my dresser, then have had to go back for it, which, I remember now, is why Mom angrily took both Isabelle's and my cell phones away.

Isabelle didn't want to be late so she wouldn't have to rush onstage at the last minute. She also wanted to see Ron Johnson before the concert started.

"If we'd left fifteen minutes earlier, we would have missed all this traffic," Dad had said.

Even now Isabelle is trying to protect me. I'm still not convinced that it was *her* fifteen minutes that made us late. If we'd left fifteen minutes earlier, she might be alive. If I hadn't changed my clothes a bunch of times, if I hadn't left my phone behind, then she might be alive. I couldn't shake the thought that she was dead because of me.

In my dream, Mom walks out of Isabelle's room and Dad follows. I can't believe that Isabelle isn't coming with us. Suddenly I am gasping for breath. I am begging my parents to stay there with Isabelle and me.

"We need you to put a stop to this, Giz," Dad says in his best forceful army voice.

"We're going to have Izzie's service without you," Mom says. "You're not going to be able to say a proper goodbye."

Mom wheels Dad away.

I rush out behind them, begging them to return, but they disappear. They are gone.

The hospital hallway stretches out like a long tunnel ahead of me. It's completely empty now. There is no one there but me.

I am still gasping for breath. I can't believe my parents have just walked away from both Isabelle and me.

I keep shouting for my parents.

I keep shouting for Isabelle.

"Come back! Come back!" I yell.

"Hi." The redheaded nurse is looking down at me when I wake up. Her hair looks like it's on fire, each individual strand, part of a fading glow.

"Welcome back, honey," she says. "It's awfully nice to see you."

CHAPTER 16

DAD TAKES HIS *US Army Survival Manual* everywhere he goes. Not the real thing but a reprint, the kind you can buy in any bookstore. The real one he left behind in the Kuwaiti desert after coming home from Operation Desert Storm, the first Iraq War.

Dad and Uncle Patrick left Haiti to go to boarding school in upstate New York around the same time that Grandma Sandrine, Mom, and Aunt Leslie moved to Miami, after their father, Grandpa Napo, died.

Dad always knew that he wanted to be a lawyer, but after his high school graduation, he saw a TV ad for the US Army and decided to enlist. The recruiter put a rush on his green card application, and soon after he signed the papers, Dad was shipped off to boot camp.

A few weeks after Dad finished boot camp, Operation Desert Storm broke out and Dad was deployed to Kuwait. He didn't let Mom, Uncle Patrick, or his parents know that he'd joined the army until it was too late for them to do anything about it.

If not for being so worried about him, Grandpa Marcus and Grandma Régine would have never spoken to him again. When he was deployed overseas, even though he wasn't allowed to tell them exactly where he was, they'd send him care packages filled with candy bars and clean underwear, through an army post office address, every week. They'd also send him books—law books, novels—anything that could take his mind off whatever he was doing over there. Not that this was so easy, he wrote in what Isabelle and I called his "war letters."

Nothing is easy here, he would write to Mom in almost every letter. *I can't live without you.*

"What was he expecting?" Isabelle would say, less sympathetically after the separation announcement. "He was in a war after all."

Dad's time in the desert lasted only four weeks. Then he caught some kind of raging eye infection, which helped him get the discharge that sent him to Mom in Miami, where he started college, then law school.

Dad and Uncle Patrick were supposed to become architects like Grandpa Marcus, the kind of architects who would rebuild Haiti. That was the deal they'd made with Grandpa Marcus when he sent them to boarding school in the United States. Instead, Dad fell in love with the law and he stayed in love with Mom. Uncle Patrick fell in love with music and with a whole bunch of women until he met Alejandra.

Almost nothing worked out the way Grandpa Marcus and Grandma Régine thought it would, except Izzie and me, their only grandchildren.

After he left the army, Dad mainly concentrated on his studies and on Mom. He tried to leave everything from the army behind, except his army pals, and the copy of the survival guide he always carried with him. I bet it was even with him the day of the crash.

If you take a poll of people who survive anything, Dad likes to say, you'll find that most of them have an iron will. Before all this, I would have never thought of myself as having an iron will.

When Dad comes into my hospital room with Mom and Grandma Régine and Grandpa Marcus and Aunt Leslie and Uncle Patrick, I can feel the iron will etched on my face.

"And she wakes up on the fifth day," Dad shouts. "We can improvise this thing now. Gizzie's going to be okay."

Everyone lines up, or wheels up, in a half circle around me, then they each take turns asking me the same questions.

"How are you feeling?"

"Are you hungry?"

"Are you thirsty?"

Before my family came in, the head duck doctor said I could have water and a few creamy foods, some soup. The redheaded nurse started me with applesauce.

"Make room, make room," Dad says. It's the strongest I have heard his voice since the crash.

Uncle Patrick pushes Dad's wheelchair forward. Dad has his fighting face on, even though his body doesn't quite match it now.

"Let's go home soon," Dad tells me.

"I don't think you get to decide, Dave," Aunt Leslie says.

They all start talking at the same time. This makes me feel like I'm at one of our loud Thanksgiving dinners where everyone talks and no one listens. Rather than being awful, the way it usually is when everyone wants to have a say, this time it's kind of nice, though not nice enough for me to want it to go on forever.

Besides, my head starts to hurt and I feel queasy, like I've just jumped off someplace really high and am floating down in slow motion towards the ground.

"Please," I say. I think I'm yelling but it comes out as a whisper. "I'm tired."

The inside of my mouth feels stuffed and dry, like it's filled with cotton balls. Rather than being quiet, my family cheers. Dad cheers the loudest of everyone.

"That's what I'm talking about," he says. *"Se sa!"*

After the duck doctor and his ducklings come back and clear the room, I remember the reason Mom and Dad want to be out of the hospital so soon. They want to have a funeral service for Isabelle and they don't want to do it without me.

"You might just be able to make your sister's funeral," the head duck doctor says.

"Don't sound so cheerful about it," I say, now continuing out loud the running conversation I've been having with him in my head.

He flinches, but he also looks proud after hearing my raspy voice.

Still, I can tell that he's also embarrassed. He got too used to me not talking back.

CHAPTER 17

THE ROOM SEEMS a lot brighter later that afternoon when I am supposed to get up and stand on my feet. Suddenly the things around me—the glass bricks on the wall, my painting from Jean Michel—finally seem more real than the world in my head.

Somehow I am going to get out of this bed and walk. Even if I walk just a few feet, to the wheelchair. I am going to take my first few steps outside of my dreams.

I am also seeing everybody in a new way. Their mouths are no longer mute, their faces no longer sad. Everyone is now in Technicolor, a whole range of pink, blue, grey, and green hospital gowns and scrubs.

Everyone is smiling. I am actually smiling, too. I'm happy to see the back of the bed rise, happy to see the railing collapse as it's being pushed down by the head duck doctor, who looks very pleased with himself.

He looks like he wants to channel Victor Frankenstein and scream, "She's alive! She's alive!"

He lowers the bed as far down as it can go, to a place where it seems possible for my feet to reach the ground. My leg muscles tense up and my body starts shaking. My head feels like it's spinning even before my feet hit the ground.

"Easy, easy," the head duck doctor says.

I can actually feel the ground. It feels cold, wet, snow cold.

Miraculously, as the head duck keeps saying, I have no broken bones.

The redheaded nurse rushes forward and drops a pair of slippers in front of me. My slippers from home. No, Isabelle's black satin slippers that someone mistook for mine. Mine are white and made with terry cloth. Whoever picked the slippers to bring to the hospital might have been thinking that taking these first steps in Isabelle's slippers would inspire me.

I have to fight to stay upright, I tell myself, so I can go to Isabelle's service. And right then, a bolt of what feels like lightning shoots through me from the bottom of my feet to the top of my head. My ears start ringing. I hear gasps around the room. I hear Grandma Régine shout, "Jesus, Marie, Joseph!"

"You go, Gizzie!" Dad calls, with a voice that sounds stronger than his body might ever be again.

I fall backwards, into the duck doctor's arms. I will have to learn his name. I'll have to write him a letter one day. A thank-you note like the kind Mom always made me and Isabelle write when we got any kind of gift. A gift is never truly yours until you say thank you, Mom likes to say. The gift the head duck and the others have given me is part of my life back. How do you write a thank-you note for that?

The head duck cradles my back until the ducklings and the redheaded nurse rush forward to help hold me up.

"Give her some space," he says.

I look into his coffee-colored eyes and realize how determined they are. He's mouthing words to me that the rest of the room can't hear.

"Are you a runner?" he asks.

Is he worried that I'm going to start running? Away from him and everyone here?

"I don't run," I say, meaning I won't run away. I won't flee. I won't give up.

"So you don't jog or anything?"

Couldn't think of the last time I did. But Isabelle did jog, mostly for her PE class, the one where she and Ron Johnson became friends.

"Do you exercise at all?" he asks.

"I swim," I whisper.

"Not for the next couple of weeks," he says, "because anything that raises your heart rate can increase the speed at which blood flows to your brain, which would not be a good thing."

"Okay," I say, pretending I fully understand him.

"Do you like movies?" he asks.

"Yes."

"You won't be able to watch any for a while. No tablet or computer screens, either."

But those things don't raise heart rates, I want to say. Or they might.

"You like reading?" he asks.

"Yes."

"No reading for a while," he says.

"Okay," I say. He is starting to sound like a broken record.

"I hear you like to draw," he says.

Let me guess, I'm not going to be able to draw for a while.

"No drawing," he says.

And she wins . . .

"There is some good news, though," he says.

I really want to find out what that good news is.

"Dark glasses, shades, what do you kids call them? You'll be wearing shades now whenever you go out."

"For how long?" I ask.

Most of my voice still gets caught in my throat, and I'm not sure how much of what I'm saying he hears. He makes me repeat myself, then says, "For as long as it takes. A couple of weeks or so. And I have to tell you that if you hit your head again, it wouldn't be a good thing."

Okay, then.

He's been holding me so long now that I feel like we're dancing some kind of slow waltz of horror. I want him to help me go back to bed so I can lie down and rest, except I want to get out of here. I want to leave this place. I don't want Isabelle's funeral service to happen without me.

"Go ahead," the head duck says. "You can do this."

I'm not sure what the "this" is that I can do. Is it taking one step? Two steps? Is it walking out of the room and never looking back?

I let my feet sink into Isabelle's slippers. Isabelle would want me to stay on my feet. She would want me to attend her funeral. Actually, she'd probably ask for her slippers back. I want to take that step as much as I wanted to move my toes not so long ago.

"I can do this," I mouth to the head duck. I am now heaving, sweating, breathless, trying to stay upright. I can do this, I keep telling myself. I will do it.

The head duck offers me his arm. I don't just reach for it, I grab it and let my hand slip through the crook of his elbow.

"Here you go," he mouths back. I press one side of my body against his, taking some of the weight off my feet.

"You can trust your legs," he says. "It's okay."

At first I slide more than I raise my legs. I feel no parasitic drag. Then my neck starts to feel like it's strong enough to hold my wobbly head again. My breath slows down, too, and I feel less afraid.

I raise my legs, and Isabelle's slippers come up with them. They are my propellers, my engines, the way Isabelle was.

I take a first step. Then another. Then another. I feel the head duck's hand slip away from mine. I take a few more steps, until I'm standing next to Mom and Dad and the rest of my family who have come out to see me take my first steps, this time on my own, without my sister.

Everyone is clapping by the time I reach them. I'm close enough to smell the hospital on both my parents, the alcohol swabs, the citrus-scented soaps, the strong antibacterial gels. I smell the same way.

"Let's go home," I say as Mom raises her hands to her face and sobs in her fingers.

"Not so fast, baby bird," the head duck says.

CHAPTER 18

LAST HALLOWEEN, ON a Saturday morning, Dad found a small brown owl in our backyard, by the pool, under our avocado tree. He called us all out of bed to see it, wobbling back and forth on our deck. It looked like its wing had been broken.

I had never seen an owl before, except in pictures, but the flat face and super-massive eyes gave it away.

We stood at a safe distance and watched it struggle to lift itself off the ground, only to fall back down again. Mom was worried that it would hurt itself even more if we allowed it to keep trying to fly, but she ordered us not to get too close so it wouldn't bite us. The only thing left to do was to call the Miami wildlife center.

We stood there and watched the owl flap its wings again and again. It could not get off the ground. It would occasionally stop to rest, bobbing its head up and down, as if it couldn't believe what was happening.

Dad thought it had fallen out of its nest in the avocado tree and had wounded itself when it landed on the ground.

Being nocturnal, it probably couldn't even see us, Dad said. Thank goodness it didn't fall into the pool.

"We have owls in our avocado tree?" Isabelle asked. "What else is up there? Bats?"

"Do you want to climb the tree with me and find out?" I asked.

This is what we would have done when we were little.

Isabelle shot me a horrified look. She thought it was too creepy that this owl had landed on our back porch, on Halloween of all times.

When the man from the wildlife center arrived, he said that we were smart not to have gotten too close to the owl, because it could have bitten us pretty hard if it felt it was in danger. It turns out that our owl was a type of burrowing owl that was on the endangered species list in the United States. The fine for hurting or killing one was ten thousand dollars.

"Is there a reward for finding one?" Isabelle asked him.

"Unfortunately no," the man said.

Unlike other owls, burrowing owls are pretty small in general and they're not strictly nocturnal, he explained. They stay active during the day when they gather food and burrow in holes in the ground.

Even though she hadn't seemed that enthusiastic about the owl, every day after that, for at least a couple of weeks, I saw Isabelle checking the deck and around the pool after she woke up.

One night after dinner, a few weeks later, she looked out on the deck and said, "I wonder where our owl is?"

"In a better place," Dad said.

"Don't joke about that," she said, as if she thought he was saying the owl was dead.

"I mean the safer place that is the wildlife center," he explained.

"We should visit it sometime," she said, though we never visited or even called to find out what had become of it.

Now I am like that owl. I am heading someplace that is like home, but not really home.

Our house would never be the same place it had been that evening, when we all got into Dad's car and left for the concert.

CHAPTER 19

MOM AND DAD are discharged from the hospital later that afternoon. It's been five days since the car crash, but it feels like it's been five years.

I have to show the head duck that I can follow instructions before he can let me out in the next couple of days. I have to follow his fingers back and forth with my eyeballs. I have to count backward and forward, then repeat the days of the week and the months of the year. I have to pass a vision test and get a prescription for sun and glare glasses. I have to organize word lists. I have to solve math problems verbally and show that I can remember important moments from my life. I have to tell him and some other duck neurologists the names of my teachers and friends. I even have to sing the US national anthem to a speech therapist. I have to be told over and over to let my parents know if I ever feel depressed or suicidal.

Every now and then, pain randomly shoots through different parts of my still-black-and-blue body, but I choose to ignore it. I am going to pretend that on a scale of one to a billion, I am a zero.

The fact that I'll have Aunt Leslie as my own in-house pediatrician reassures the head duck that I'll be "compliant" once I'm discharged. I hear him tell Aunt Leslie that she should observe me closely and rush me right back here if needed.

"You do know that your aunt and I went to medical school together, don't you?" he asks, grinning at her, like an employee trying to impress his supervisor.

I didn't know.

My parents' doctors order them to stay home and rest before Isabelle's service. Aunt Leslie agrees that any trips back and forth would be too much for them.

Instead, Aunt Leslie and Grandma Régine come to visit.

"Where are the men?" I ask. "Fishing?"

"You *are* back," Aunt Leslie says.

"Are you sure Mom and Dad aren't staying away on purpose?" I ask Aunt Leslie.

"Why would you say that?" Grandma Régine moves closer to the railing and looks directly into my eyes.

"I don't know," I say, but I do know.

I know it's crazy, but I'm worried that my parents might be angry with me for not dying, for hanging around to constantly remind them of Isabelle.

"I had to threaten them to keep them away," Aunt Leslie says. "I got all doctor on them and told them to stay home and rest. They lost Izzie here. They nearly lost you. Coming in and out of here is not the best thing for them."

This makes sense logically, but I can't help thinking back to the last time I was hospitalized here. Izzie and I were ten years old. I had a terrible case of food poisoning after eating badly cooked fish at a seafood restaurant. Isabelle was fine but she insisted on being hospitalized with me, a wish my parents only partially granted. She was pulled out of school, where she wasn't concentrating anyway, and was allowed to spend the three days with me, but she had to go home at night and sleep in her own bed. My parents, though, took turns spending those nights in a cot next to my bed. I know that if I ask either Aunt Leslie or Grandma Régine to spend the night in the hospital with me, they will. But it's not the same.

Anyway, when I get out, just like Mom and Dad, I want to stay out of this place for good. I never want to come back.

Grandma Régine steps away from my bed. She looks preoccupied. Like she has many other places to be. I know there's a lot happening outside this hospital room. My parents must feel like they can finally make arrangements for Isabelle's funeral. They believe I can make it there. Aunt Leslie and Grandma Régine are taking care of my parents, too. All while trying to live a fragment of the lives they had before.

Aunt Leslie lets me talk to Mom and Dad on her cell phone, but they don't keep me long. They seem worried about tiring me out.

"Make sure you get plenty of rest," Mom says, as if I had some other choice.

I ask Dad about Dessalines and he chokes up. He coughs to cover up his sobs.

When Uncle Patrick comes by later that night, we talk about his new artist. Uncle Patrick has just signed Emeline to his new label, Gemelita Iz, the label he's just started with Alejandra. He'd hoped to work with Isabelle one day, he says, either as a producer or songwriter. Gemelita Iz might be as close as he ever gets.

"I know how much Isabelle loved Emeline's music," he says, "so after Isabelle"—he stops himself and takes a breath—"after things happened, I started listening to Emeline around the clock, and both Alejandra and I fell in love with her voice."

Emeline does have a powerful voice, a voice that can cradle and soothe you after you've been hurt, but can also make you get up and dance when you never thought you could. Her voice is high at times and deep at others. It sounds like every voice you've ever missed and longed to hear in your entire life.

"Emeline made me laugh," Uncle Patrick says. "She made me dance. She made me cry. She made us pray. I had to have her on our new label, and I am so glad she said yes."

I am glad, too. Isabelle would have been ecstatic, over the moon. The idea of three of her favorite people making music together would have thrilled her to no end.

After Uncle Patrick leaves, I can't sleep. I can only think of Isabelle. Was it a failure of twindom that I didn't figure out all by myself that she was gone? Or maybe I didn't want to feel it. I didn't want to believe it.

That time when I fell down the stairs, Isabelle was sitting in English class when her head began to hurt. It was a different kind of pain than a headache, and it came on so suddenly—like a blow to the head—that even before the nurse sent for her, she knew I'd hit my head.

Sometimes we'd have the same dreams. We were tourists in each other's heads. Our dreams were like bad student horror films, full of loose unconnected plots. They were extreme adventures. We would dream ourselves going over Niagara Falls in a barrel, floating aimlessly in a hot-air balloon over a shattered post-earthquake Port-au-Prince. We would dream ourselves trying to out-ski an avalanche, swatting a beehive off our bodies with our bare hands.

Every now and then, we'd have one calm and reassuring recurring dream. We would see ourselves swimming with a pod of rare pink dolphins, in an endless river, deep in the Brazilian rain forest. We were both lucid dreamers. We knew when we were dreaming and could always control our dreams. Maybe Isabelle already knew that her life would be short. She tried to get as much living in as possible. Even when she was asleep.

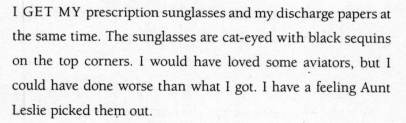

CHAPTER 20

I GET MY prescription sunglasses and my discharge papers at the same time. The sunglasses are cat-eyed with black sequins on the top corners. I would have loved some aviators, but I could have done worse than what I got. I have a feeling Aunt Leslie picked them out.

These are my discharge orders: I can't read or watch TV. I can't look at my laptop or any other kind of screen. If I do, I risk hurting my brain.

The head duck says I should expect to feel nauseated now and then. I might also get dizzy and forget things. He says I should wear the sunglasses whenever I'm outside. He says I might feel tired a lot and be extremely sensitive to noise and light. He says I might have mood swings and might have trouble sleeping.

Even with all that, I'm so ready to go home that if they don't let me out, I'll escape.

My departure day turns into an almost celebration. Grandpa Marcus brings in a large bouquet of daisies from Ms. Volcy, the principal at Morrison High.

"This is only a sample," Grandpa Marcus says as he takes Jean Michel's painting down from the wall. "Everyone is happy that you are going home."

I imagine my parents putting on their church clothes, getting ready for Isabelle's service that same morning.

Before I can put on the dress that Grandma Régine has in the garment bag, I have to get a final checkup from the head duck doctor. This time, when he walks into the room, alone, without his ducklings, Grandma Régine and Grandpa Marcus do not walk out.

"We like what we're seeing," the head duck says as he listens to my lungs and heart. And of course beams that penlight into the windows to my soul.

"I've discussed all this with your parents and with your aunt Leslie," he says and lingers on Aunt Leslie's name. "You have to take it easy and get lots of rest. Don't overexert yourself after the service today. You can see how you feel when you get home, but you should be able to go back to school in a few weeks."

"Yes, sir," I say.

I want to hug him, but I just add, "Thank you."

My voice is still scratchy, still way too deep, and I'm not sure he hears me until he says, "You're welcome. Now let me go and sign your paperwork."

He seems like a different person than when I was under. Not just an arrogant duck, and not that bad looking, either. He looks younger now, hipper. There's suddenly something very self-assured, very dapper—rather than dabbler—about him.

For the first time since he's been taking care of me, I notice the name embroidered on his lab coat: Dr. Emmanuel Aidoo. Under his name, in the same dark blue lettering, is the word *Neurology*.

When Dr. Aidoo leaves, Grandpa Marcus walks out with him so I can get dressed.

In the garment bag Grandma Régine is holding is a knee-length black dress with the tag still attached. I've lost some weight. The bell-shaped dress is so loose that it hangs like a tent on my body. Grandma Régine walks over to the wall and picks up my necklace. I sit back down on the bed; she unlatches it and puts it around my neck.

Grandpa Marcus knocks on the door before coming back in.

"*J'apporte ces choses à la voiture*," Grandpa Marcus says while gathering my things, including Ms. Volcy's daisies. "I'm taking these to the car."

It seems like Grandpa Marcus and Grandma Régine have worked out everything for our trip to the funeral parlor.

After Grandpa Marcus leaves, the redheaded nurse comes in with a wheelchair and helps me into it. She's wearing pink scrubs with a bunch of cartoon characters, which I don't remember her having worn before. She motions for me to walk over to the chair, then ceremoniously bows as though it were a throne.

I fall too fast into my throne, and there's no cushion for my behind. The redheaded nurse's concerned gasp sounds sweet to me. I am going home, but not before attending Isabelle's service.

"You can put on your sunglasses," the redheaded nurse says. And I do.

"You look like a 1960s movie star," she says.

Before they start protecting me from the glare of the world, my sunglasses shield me from the world of the hospital hallway, from the other nurses—including the hunky bearded male nurse—waving goodbye. I don't get to fully see the other patients turning their heads to get one final envious look at me. The glasses also hide the tears bubbling up in my eyes.

Outside, Grandma Régine, the redheaded nurse, and I wait for Grandpa Marcus to pull up. Grandpa Marcus is driving Mom's grey SUV.

When Grandpa Marcus pulls up in front of us, I panic.

A car.

A road.

If I hit my head again, I might die.

My eyes quickly adjust to the sunglasses. I pull myself up and slide into the second row of Mom's car. Grandma Régine waits for me to settle in before she gets in the front seat next to Grandpa Marcus. The redheaded nurse keeps waving goodbye as we pull away.

"Do we know that nurse's name?" Grandma Régine asks Grandma Marcus in French. "It would be nice for Giselle to write her a thank-you letter."

"*Je l'ai noté*," Grandpa Marcus answers. "I took note of it. Her name is Frances Harper-Naylor."

I love you, Frances Harper-Naylor, I whisper to myself.

Grandpa Marcus stays on local roads. He's driving at least ten miles under the speed limit.

Isabelle and I were supposed to stage out of our learner's permits and get our licenses in a few weeks, just before our seventeenth birthday. Mom and Dad have both taken turns practicing with us. We were going to use Dad's car for our road tests when it was time.

Every now and then, I would hear Mom joke about our driving with Mrs. Marshall.

"Wait till they're driving by themselves," Mom would say, "then we'll be in some real trouble."

Dad would joke about intimidating the boys who'd want to ride with us.

"I'll have to pull out my old fatigues and sidearm and scare some sense into those boys," he'd say.

We are now in a residential neighborhood. Even with my sunglasses on, I can tell that Grandpa Marcus is lost. But I don't want to say anything.

Grandpa Marcus drives even more slowly for the next half hour, through more neighborhoods of single-story houses and neat lawns and the occasional schools and churches.

Finally, Grandma Régine speaks up and says, "*Nou pèdi?* Are we lost?"

Grandpa Marcus is as lost in his thoughts as he is on the road.

"Not lost, okay?" he says, picking up a little speed.

Soon, we are where we really don't want to be, but where I have fought so hard to be. We are outside Pax Villa Funeral Home and Crematorium. Isabelle is waiting for us.

CHAPTER 21

THE LAST TIME we were at Pax Villa was for Grandma Sandrine's wake. Mom decorated the chapel with Grandma Sandrine's paintings. Grandma Sandrine's silver coffin was so shiny that, while we were sitting in the front row, we could see our reflections on it.

"This coffin is going to blind God," Dad whispered during Aunt Leslie's eulogy. He was trying to make Mom laugh.

"With its beauty," Mom whispered back, wiping her tears with the back of her hand.

In one of Grandma Sandrine's lucid (or maybe not so lucid) moments, Mom had asked her to pick out a coffin from a catalog, and she chose one that was practically a mirror.

Just a few weeks ago, Isabelle was thinking about picking out a car, not a coffin. Still, as I follow Grandma Régine and

Grandpa Marcus down the carpeted hallway leading to the holding room next to the chapel, I keep hoping that Isabelle's coffin will be a nice one. The thought doesn't make sense, any more than Isabelle being dead does.

It seems that Grandma Régine and Grandpa Marcus took care of this part of things, too. When we walk into the waiting room behind the chapel, Mr. Daniels, the funeral director, greets them like old friends.

My parents, their faces locked in a kind of numbed shock, are sitting next to each other on a couch in the middle of the room, as my grandparents chat with Mr. Daniels. Dad's leg is stretched out on the wheelchair in front of him. He's wearing black sweatpants that cover the leg cast. His dark jacket is hanging over his shoulder and is partially hiding his arm cast.

Mom's dress is identical to mine—thanks to Grandma Régine. Mom's also wearing a black beret.

Alejandra, who'd left and flown back from New York, is the first to say hello.

"*¿Cómo estás, mi amor?*" she asks.

"*Más o menos,*" I answer.

"*Me gustan,*" she says, pointing to my sunglasses.

I forget that I'm wearing the sunglasses. Still, I don't take them off. They feel like another kind of safeguard now. They feel like armor, like a shield.

Aunt Leslie and Uncle Patrick, who are standing behind my parents, both call out for me to be careful when I hug Dad. They don't want me to displace his arm or trip over his leg.

It's safer to hug Mom, who, though she winces while I'm hugging her, still manages to say, "You look so nice. You do."

Mr. Daniels, a large man who is still swimming in his loose black suit, walks over to us.

"I'm so sorry for your loss," he says, grasping my hand. He points to a spot on the couch next to Mom, as if suggesting for me to go sit there. But I just stand where I am and wait to hear what he'll say next.

"Should I bring her in now?" he says to no one in particular.

Oh, please bring her in, I want to say. But bring her in the way she was before we left that evening for the concert. Bring her in to tell us that this was all a joke, a hoax she's been planning for weeks. A joke that everyone else is in on except me.

This would be her best practical joke ever. It would beat her silly April Fool's pranks of scraping out the insides of minty Oreos and replacing the cream with toothpaste, or greasing our toilet seats with Vaseline.

Mr. Daniels leaves, then comes back with two assistants who wheel the coffin in. And what a coffin it is! It's a coffin that Isabelle would not only have liked, but loved.

Mr. Daniels doesn't need to explain the coffin, but he does. I can tell that one way he tries to comfort families is by describing to them what they're already seeing.

"Just as you requested," he says, turning to my grandparents, "this is a picture coffin, made of a hundred percent recycled clapboard, honeycomb based. It's on loan for the service. She won't be cremated in it."

Those details are obviously important to him. And to us, too. I didn't realize that Isabelle's body was going to be here. I didn't even know she was going to be cremated. Both our parents have it in their wills that they want to be cremated, something they'd sat Isabelle and me down and told us, something that none of their parents had agreed with.

Dad and Grandma Régine have argued about it a bunch of times. Grandma Régine wants a grave, a headstone, a place to visit and lay flowers. Dad believes that it's about taking up space, using up more of the world's resources even after you've left it.

I'm sure that if Mom wasn't too sad to speak up, she'd remind everyone, just as she and Dad had told Isabelle and me, that on both sides of the family, going back several generations, parents have never gone to cemeteries to see their children being buried. If Dad had died in the car crash, for example, Grandpa Marcus and Grandma Régine wouldn't have stood by his open grave and watched as his body was lowered into the earth.

They would have gone to the chapel, or the church, then would have gone home to wait for everyone else to return from the cemetery for the repast. Later they would have visited the filled-in grave, but parents were not supposed to witness their children sinking into the ground. So my parents were not going to bury Isabelle.

The picture coffin is pink, with giant hibiscus painted all over it. I've never seen a coffin like this, and from the way my parents' eyes pop, neither have they.

"We thought Izzie would like it for this little while," Grandma Régine says in her most Parisian French.

Usually this is the kind of moment that might lead to a full-on Creole brawl between Dad and his parents.

"You mean you like it," Dad might have said.

Then Grandma Régine's lips would have curled with hurt and her eyes would have watered in distress, and Grandpa Marcus would have had to come to her rescue by saying something like, "I know you're a grown man, but this is not how we talk to our mothers where I come from." And Dad would have stopped talking out of respect, but only for a minute. Then Dad would pick things up again and complain some more. Grandma Régine would get her courage back and say, "I'm sorry to have displeased you again." And Mom would have to referee and say, "Can we take a breather, please?" Then Dad would lean towards Mom and say, "I don't get why they always do this."

And Mom would say, "Because you always do what you're doing right now."

Isabelle and I would of course be captivated by all this. First of all because it would happen in a mix of Creole, French, and English. And even some Spanish if Alejandra was around. Boyer family fights were like fights at the United Nations.

"Wow, people still fight with their parents into old age," Isabelle would joke, and this would take some, but not all, of the edge off.

But there's no such fight in the funeral home that day. Dad is clearly not happy but he can live with the coffin. After all, this is not the only strange coffin the family's ever seen. Grandma Sandrine's was also "unique." And if funerals are for the dead, rather than the people who come to see the dead, then Isabelle would have loved this coffin.

"Cool," she might have said, just as she had about Grandma Sandrine's coffin. "Different."

"We'll open it now," Mr. Daniels says.

The way he says "we" makes me think he'll need all of us to do it, because it's going be such a physically impossible task. Like picking up some kind of massive boulder. But all he does is turn his back to us and raise the lid, and there she is.

At first I don't move an inch. I just look at her from behind my dark glasses, from a few feet away. Mom screams out Isabelle's name and Dad reaches out and wraps his good arm around her. Uncle Patrick turns away after one glance as Aunt Leslie sobs on his chest.

Alejandra reaches for my hand, but doesn't quite make it. I am watching my parents on the couch, with their arms around each other. The way they look, it's hard to imagine they will ever come apart again, not even for a moment, much less for the rest of their lives.

I take a few steps closer to the coffin.

Up close, I can see why Grandma Régine chose it. It's girly in a way that Isabelle liked to be, but would never openly admit. The inside is lined in pink silk and under her head is a matching pillow. Isabelle looks whole. There's no sign of any cuts or bruises under the layers of cinnamon-colored stage makeup covering her face.

Everyone says this about the dead, but she does look like she's sleeping. Even after all this time, and given everything her body's been through, she still looks like herself. I keep thinking that if I nudge her, she might wake up.

Just like the evening of the crash, she's dressed in one of her formal orchestra uniforms, a white blouse and pencil skirt. The night of the concert, she also wanted to wear one of her many beaded bracelets, but no jewelry was allowed. Even the non-shiny kind was considered too distracting. She also couldn't wear anything shiny in her hair. And she's not wearing anything shiny in the coffin, either. Perhaps to best hide her wounds, what's left of her braids are bunched up together and pulled close to her face, their edges resting on her shoulders.

I don't know how she would have felt about the uniform.

"Does this mean I'll have to play the flute for all of eternity?" she might have said.

She would have liked all the makeup, though.

"Stage mask galore," she might have said.

But even with all of the makeup, she still looks like me. It's like looking at me.

After a freshman I didn't know tried to kill himself last year, I remember sitting through a suicide prevention assembly at school, and one of the things the guest psychologist said was that most people, especially young people, think that when they die, they'll be able to see everything happening around them as they are lying in their coffin.

The truth is, he said, you're not going to see those who bully you cry. You're not going to experience your parents' remorse. You're not even going to feel your friends' pain. You're never going to know what you look like dead.

Except I do. I know exactly what I look like dead. I look like Isabelle.

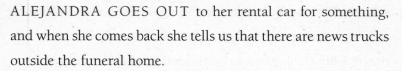

CHAPTER 22

ALEJANDRA GOES OUT to her rental car for something, and when she comes back she tells us that there are news trucks outside the funeral home.

The lobby, too, is packed with people who are waiting to get into the chapel for the service.

I walk out with Alejandra while the rest of the family helps Mom and Dad to the chapel's front row.

I wonder if Tina and Jean Michel are in the lobby. I peek out through a glass door, but don't see them in the crowd of both church and school friends waiting to get in. I think I see Dr. Aidoo standing in the lobby, in a fancy black suit, but maybe I am hallucinating him.

I don't have the heart, or energy, to walk through that crowd to find my friends or to make sure that Dr. Aidoo is really there.

Besides, just as Dr. Aidoo himself predicted, I am starting to feel a bit nauseated, blurry eyed, and dizzy. I don't want to fall and hit my head again. I ask Alejandra to take me to my parents.

I am still wearing my sunglasses as I walk to the front of the chapel. Even though Alejandra is holding on to my elbow, I feel like I'm floating towards Isabelle's beautiful coffin, which is closed and covered with camellias and birds of paradise from my parents' garden.

Next to the coffin is an easel with a large picture of Isabelle, her most recent school portrait. Under the always-too-bright school photographer's lights, her face looks a bit too shiny. She's wearing a faux pearl choker and a black, sequined blouse. Her braids hang right above her collarbone and she's smiling.

The chapel fills up quickly. Then Pastor Ben gets up to welcome us.

"A sad and incomprehensible day," he says, while tugging at his white beard.

Where is Lazarus now? I ask myself.

I can no longer disappear. I can no longer sink under. But I don't like the surface, either. At times, I feel like I'm in the hospital again, fading in and out. I adjust the sunglasses, pulling their dark tint closer to my eyes.

Uncle Patrick gets up and walks to the podium. He talks about the day Isabelle and I were born.

Mom was on bed rest her entire pregnancy. She was supposed to have a scheduled C-section, but a week before the scheduled delivery date, she began having contractions. Panicked, Dad drove her to the hospital.

"They were eager to see the world," Uncle Patrick says. "They demanded to come out."

Many things might have gone wrong, he says. We might have become entangled in each other's umbilical cords. One of us might have gobbled up all the nutrients and starved the other one in the womb. But we loved and supported each other, from day one.

Aunt Leslie gets up and talks about Isabelle's love of music, her dream of traveling the world and becoming a famous composer. She mentions how Isabelle truly believed in what Nietzsche said, that life without music is a mistake. She talks about Isabelle's sense of humor, her love of family.

I am feeling foggy again, so I force myself to stop listening. Instead, I look around the chapel.

Nearly everyone in Isabelle's life is there. Ms. Volcy, the principal, is sitting in the same row as some of the Morrison teachers. Many of Isabelle's friends from school are there, too, a few of them with their parents.

It's easy to recognize Isabelle's friends. When they're not performing, they're mostly into fangirl, fanboy wear. They are constantly broadcasting their love for their favorite musicians or bands on their ratty T-shirts. Though not today. Today they're wearing perfectly pressed sheaths, slacks, or skirts with shirts or blouses in subdued colors.

The news crews, including some of Mom's regular anchor clients, are in the back row. Their cameras are aimed right at the coffin and at us. Alejandra says that a few of the anchors sent flowers to Mom's hospital room every day, hoping to land an exclusive interview with her and Dad. My parents decided not to do any interviews.

I look in the back for Tina and Jean Michel, but I don't see them. I look for Ron Johnson. I don't see him, either.

Pastor Ben announces a selection from Isabelle's section of the school orchestra, the three guys and four girls who played the flute with Isabelle.

Isabelle's friend Lois sobs as she introduces the piece.

Isabelle had too many friends to call anyone her best friend. But if she had a best friend, it was my homeroom classmate, loud, gum-chewing, flute-playing Lois.

"We're going to play an excerpt from one of Isabelle's favorite pieces," Lois says.

Isabelle's friends play "Infernal Dance" from Stravinsky's *The Firebird*. The piece's ginormous sweep is straining, almost overwhelming them. Their tempo reminds me of the crash: silence, speed, and then *SMASH*.

It seems odd now, after my being deaf for a while, but what I loved most during Isabelle's school performances were the silences. There were both planned and unplanned silences between each movement and each piece. This made the music sound even more alive, like the silence was where the melody stopped to catch its breath.

Isabelle's friends aren't playing well because Lois, who's leading them, keeps looking down at the coffin, then at the crowd, and she is crying. Occasionally, she pulls the flute from her lips, swallows hard, then wipes the tears from her eyes. Then a breath's worth of stillness, a grand pause, or a fermata, that I wish would last forever, but is instead followed by even more sobbing from Lois and a few of the others.

The service pretty much ends after their performance. Dad asks Uncle Patrick to wheel him back to the holding room.

After Dad and Uncle Patrick leave, everyone files out row by row to come greet us. With each person who comes by, I try to figure out the connection to Isabelle.

Everyone on our block is there, including Mrs. Clifton. Isabelle liked to call Mrs. Clifton the "craft queen." Mrs. Clifton retired from her job as a flight attendant a few years back and stayed home all day watching soap operas and making crafts. She was also the block's most trusted babysitter.

Mrs. Clifton reaches up and strokes my cheeks, then

rearranges a few braids dangling over my ear. This is the first time I think about how horrible my hair must look. I can't remember brushing it, but when I touch the top of my head, my hair seems nicely parted and feels neat. I probably have Grandma Régine to thank for that.

Mrs. Clifton doesn't say anything to me, and I appreciate that. I don't feel like talking. Our mailman, Hilton, stops by. So does Moy, Dad's commissioner friend. Our housekeeper, Josiane, says hi, too. She's with her husband.

Our pediatrician, Dr. Rosemay, also stops by. With no offense to Aunt Leslie, Dr. Rosemay is probably the most elegant doctor in the entire world. Even though she has patients ranging from newborns to teenagers, she wears low-cut dresses and long red nails and speaks with a combo French/Creole accent that you could listen to all day long.

"I'm sorry for your loss," almost everyone—including Dr. Rosemay—says. It's as if they've all been given a script. "Please let me know if there's anything I can do," she says.

Dr. Rosemay looks as though she's fighting the urge to examine me, right then and there. When she holds my wrists, I swear she's secretly taking my pulse.

I know she wants to see my eyes, so I raise the glasses so she can.

"Dr. Rosemay came to see you a couple of times in the hospital," Mom says, interrupting our staring contest. "She's been in touch with Dr. Aidoo and she'll be taking over most of your care."

"I don't remember," I tell Dr. Rosemay.

"I'm not surprised," she says.

When Isabelle's friend Lois comes by, like Dr. Rosemay, she stands with me longer than she does any other member of my family. Everyone else has managed to act as if they couldn't see it, but Lois can't help herself.

"You look just like her." She stops the greeting line completely by blurting out the obvious.

A few people gasp, but she is telling the truth. An uncomfortable truth, but the truth nonetheless. No one will ever forget Isabelle as long as I'm walking around with her body and her face. My sister is dead and I am her ghost.

More kids from school walk by. Some of them I don't know. Then finally, I see Ron Johnson.

Ron Johnson is wearing a light blue seersucker suit with a striped tie. I recognize his retro tortoiseshell glasses, the ones whose lenses turn even darker than mine in the sun. He looks almost bug-eyed standing there, as if waiting for me to say something to him. I'd seen the same slouched posture in the pictures Isabelle had taken of him.

"Hello," I say.

"Hello," he answers.

The first time I heard Ron Johnson's name, two whales had

beached themselves not far from our school, and while jogging one morning, Isabelle's PE class came across them.

Of all the people on the beach that morning, including the PE teacher, Ron Johnson was the only one who knew what to do. From their color (black and coal grey) and size (between 2,200 and 6,600 pounds), he could tell that they were short-finned pilot whales that had lost their way and wandered into the shallow water, then onto the beach. Ron Johnson told the teacher to call the wildlife center, then ordered everyone, including passersby, to keep away. Even after the rest of the PE class returned to school, Ron and Isabelle stayed behind and watched the wildlife people haul the whales back out to sea.

That night, after the whales returned to sea, Isabelle came home with a glow. The fact that she'd been in the sun all day was part of it, but she also had the excitement of a new love interest.

Ron Johnson was not the type of guy she would have typically liked, but she was drawn to people with special talents. Ron Johnson and the whales were a powerful enough combo to make her miss a mock SAT test that everyone in our year was supposed to take that afternoon.

"You know, Giz," she told me when she got home that night. "Ron says those kinds of whales stick together no matter what. If one of them had died, they both might have died."

I was only half listening.

"I'll take the next SAT practice test," she said, trying to calm my unspoken concern. "People take these tests all the time, but how many times does anyone get to see what Ron and I have seen?"

"So it's Ron and I?"

"Would you prefer me and Ron?" she asked and laughed.

Some TV reporters had spent the day on the beach with them, she said. Because she and Ron were skipping classes, they'd avoided the cameras. Now I wished I had hours of video of the two of them, full proof of what I'd suspected, that before she died, my sister had fallen in love.

That night, she showed me dozens of pictures of the whales on her phone. Ron Johnson was in the foreground of some of the pictures. The whales had moved him so much that in almost every other picture, he had his glasses off and was wiping his eyes.

Now, in the chapel, Ron Johnson takes off his glasses and wipes his eyes with his jacket sleeve.

"Can I give you a hug?" he asks.

A few people have hugged me already. Most people are aware that squeezing my body at this moment in time is not a good idea, but some tried without even asking. I wanted to push most of them away. I even thought of joining Dad in the back

room, but I don't want to miss any of my final minutes with
Isabelle. I don't want to leave her sooner than I have to. I also
don't mind if Ron Johnson hugs me.

I open my arms and Ron Johnson leans in. His body feels
sandy and damp. His hair smells like seaweed and his face is
shiny with shea butter sunscreen. He smells like the beach at
dawn. He smells like Isabelle.

Ron Johnson does not squeeze me. He doesn't even hold me.
I hold him, gently, carefully, like he is my sister in her most
vulnerable, most wounded, nearly dead state.

"You don't smell like her," he whispers.

"You do," I say.

He is shivering a little when he pulls away. Then he grabs
both my hands.

I remember the pictures Isabelle showed me that night, and
I say, "Pilot whales."

Even behind my glasses and his, I can see a spark of recognition in his eyes. He smiles cautiously, like someone who's just
been initiated into a dark and secret club. Then he lets go of my
hands and walks away.

I watch him walk away, framed by the stained-glass windows on the chapel walls. I remember how much Isabelle and
I both loved those sixteenth-century Mexican cathedrals. I
remember how much we loved every cathedral we'd ever
been in.

Grandpa Marcus is the head architect in a team that's building a new cathedral in Port-au-Prince. Last summer he took us to visit the site on a hilltop that could be seen from so many places in the city that the cathedral's main steeple will be used as a lighthouse.

Isabelle and I were Grandpa Marcus's last hope of having another architect in the family. We, like Grandpa Marcus, had become so intrigued by cathedrals that during our visits, Grandpa Marcus would take us to see most of the signature cathedrals in Haiti.

"Yes, Guanajuato has some magnificent cathedrals," Grandpa Marcus would tell us, "but I don't think the Guanajuato saints hear as many urgent prayers as ours do."

Grandpa Marcus would lecture us for hours while driving from one Haitian town to the next, over belly-churning roads, up and down steep, ragged hills. He was always his own driver and Grandma Régine his navigator.

"A garden can easily become its own kind of cathedral," he'd say. "Any healing place can be. Any place where people can come out of the sun, and wind, and rain, and just sit down and cry."

"Grandpère, you're going to put yourself out of a job talking like that," Isabelle would tell him.

"There's no way we can outdo all that nature has already designed so well," Grandpa Marcus would say.

Dad waits until nearly everyone is gone to come back into the chapel. Mr. Daniels wheels him in. Jean Michel, Tina and Pastor Ben, Mr. and Mrs. Marshall come and sit in the pew behind us. Jean Michel's parents join them. Jean Michel looks like a perfect combination of his parents. He has his Chinese Jamaican mother's button nose and his French Canadian father's large saucer eyes.

Tina reaches over and squeezes my shoulder. I've missed her so much that I almost don't know what to do.

"It's time for us to take her away," Mr. Daniels finally tells Mom and Dad.

We could have all sat there for a million years. Instead we watch as the funeral home staff wheel the coffin out towards the crematorium.

Isabelle is going to be cremated and later we'll decide where to scatter her ashes.

I hear Mom scream. Then Aunt Leslie. I close my eyes so I don't see the coffin go through the chapel door one final time. I have been saying goodbye to Isabelle ever since our hands were pried apart in Dad's car.

I always imagined that if our fortunes were read, I would be half of Isabelle's future. One of our unspoken dreams was to go on a road trip, just the two of us. One day we might have fully become women. We might have had careers, offices, apartments. Even if we lived in different cities, we might have ended up talking to each other on the phone a bunch of times a day. We might have traveled around the world together. We might have kept dreaming each other's dreams. We might have loved each other even more carefully, more gently.

I've been saying goodbye to all of that since the crash.

I've been saying goodbye all along.

CHAPTER 23

WHEN WE PULL up to the house, Dessalines is peeking out from behind the glass on the side of the front door. I call for him as soon as Josiane opens the door. Dessalines wraps himself around my legs and curls up there like a boot I want to keep on forever.

I take off my glasses so they don't scare him. Josiane bends down and picks him up. We walk over to the living room couch and she puts him in my lap. Dessalines licks my face as though it's covered in tuna oil, and I'm so wrapped up in him that at first I don't notice anything else.

The house is filled with flowers, balloons, and teddy bears. Josiane tells me that some of these things came from total strangers who'd read about Isabelle's death in the newspapers or had heard about us on the news. The island between the kitchen and dining room is covered with cards: open cards lined up in rows, probably by Grandma Régine.

Dessalines stays in my lap for a minute or so, then leaps across the coffee table to where my parents are sitting: Dad with his legs stretched out in front of him and Mom with her arms bracing her body as if to safeguard her bruised ribs. Dessalines curls up between them, and Mom and Dad take turns rubbing his back.

In the car on the way home, Grandpa Marcus, Grandma Régine, and I said very little to one another, not even to tell Grandpa Marcus that he was lost again and that everyone else was going to make it home before we did.

Grandpa Marcus had only attempted a few words.

"Izzie looked like Izzie," he said.

Now, in the house, there is even less to say.

Josiane walks to the refrigerator and pulls out some of the food people had brought by, large trays of food covered in aluminum foil, more than we could ever eat.

"Anybody hungry?" she asks.

None of us are.

Only Dessalines seems to be hungry, or maybe he's just bored with us. He rushes off to his kitchen-corner lunch.

After a while, when there's nothing else to do, Josiane carves out pieces from the different lasagnas and casseroles, and she and Grandma Régine set up a microwaved meal for us in the dining room. I can barely taste the food. I can only think of Isabelle, and how we left her all alone in that place, and how later, she would be ignited like a sparkler, then smolder into ashes.

Grandpa Marcus is sitting in Isabelle's chair, the one facing the colorful Haitian paintings on the wall. Sometimes when Isabelle was daydreaming, I'd see her staring at those green hills and blue mountains, like the ones above Grandma Régine and Grandpa Marcus's house, while quickly stuffing food in her mouth.

Mom would remind Isabelle to slow down and take her time with her food.

"There's no famine, Isabelle," Mom would say.

"Evidently," Isabelle would reply.

We all eat very slowly now, as if trying to make that meal last forever. This is what we'd have to do from now on, make things last a lot longer so we won't have to worry about what to do next.

The doorbell rings towards the end of the meal. The interruption is a relief. Both Uncle Patrick and Aunt Leslie get up to answer it. Josiane is faster and makes it to the door right before the bell rings again. She parts the curtain on the side of the door and looks out.

"*Lapolis*," she says.

"Let them in," Dad calls out, as though he's been expecting them.

Josiane opens the door and the same policewoman from the hospital walks in. This time there's a male officer with her; he's a little shorter and has a faster gait.

They look over at the table, then whisper something to Josiane.

"I'm not sure this is a good time," Mom calls out loudly.

Dad waves them over anyway.

"Are you sure?" Grandma Régine asks Dad.

"She has to talk to them," Dad says, meaning me.

The officers stand at the far end of the table, where I'm sitting. They're wearing the same black pants and long-sleeved shirts and matching stars, like the one that exploded in my head in the hospital room that day.

"Please forgive the intrusion." The female officer speaks first.

"No intrusion at all," Dad says.

He seems glad to have someone to talk to other than us.

"I'm familiar with all of you now," the female officer says, then, looking over at me, she adds, "except maybe your daughter."

I am familiar with you, I want to say, but mostly with the star on your chest.

"Again, please accept my deepest condolences," she says.

The officer next to her nods, silently adding his own condolences.

"My name is Officer Butler," she says just to me. "And this is my partner, Officer Sanchez. We're investigating the incident that led to your sister's death."

I notice she says *incident* and not *accident*.

We think what happened was not exactly an accident.

"I saw you in the hospital," Officer Butler says, keeping her eyes on me. "Officer Sanchez and I have already talked to your parents. We're here to see if there's anything you want to add. Anything we might be able to learn from you about what happened that evening. Can you please tell us what you're able to remember?"

I don't know what my parents have already told them, so I'm not sure what needs to be added. We were in a car driving to a concert, and now my sister is dead. I can't even get those few words out.

"How about we ask you a few questions?" Officer Butler pulls out a small pad from her shirt pocket and begins scribbling things down even before I can speak.

"Was there anything unusual happening before the crash?"

Everyone is staring at me now. Not just the officers, but my parents and grandparents and Aunt Leslie and Uncle Patrick and Alejandra, too.

There was a lot of traffic and a lot of cars stuck in it, but that wasn't so unusual for rush hour in Miami. I don't know what to say, so I shake my head no.

"Have you ever seen the car that hit you? I mean before that day," she says.

I had never seen that car before, so, even though it hurt a little bit, I shake my head no for that one, too.

The way the questions are going, it seems like they already know something I don't. It almost seems like I should be questioning them. Were there unusual things happening that I hadn't noticed? Was I supposed to have seen that red minivan before?

"The young woman driving the red minivan was a student at your school," Officer Butler says. "She was enrolled there up to the night of the incident."

She's speaking so slowly that I think maybe I'm still deaf. Am I actually hearing those words or am I reading her lips?

"Morrison?" I ask.

"That's where you go to school, isn't it?" she asks.

Who at school would want to hurt us enough to ram a car into us?

"Are you familiar with a student from your school named Gloria Carlton?" Officer Sanchez takes over the questioning. He speaks slowly, too, except his face edges closer with every syllable, before he pulls back again.

Morrison is one of the smaller charter high schools. Still, over six hundred kids go there. I don't know all of them.

"What grade is she in?" I ask, as if this would matter. Was she more likely to want to kill us if she was a freshman than a senior?

"She's relatively new to your school," Officer Sanchez says. "Ninth grade. Midyear transfer."

Why is he calling it *my* school, as though I own it?

"I don't know her," I say.

"She was the one driving the car," he says. "We're just trying to gather all the facts."

Who is this Gloria Carlton, and why would she want to hurt us? It doesn't sound like she's even old enough to be driving.

"I didn't see the driver's face," I say. "All I saw were the lights."

"That's understandable," Officer Butler says.

Before Mom had mentioned it, I thought we might have been hit by someone older. An old man who'd had a heart attack at the wheel. An old lady who was driving way past her ninetieth birthday. A drunk with an expired license. I never thought it could be someone close to my age.

"Gloria Carlton was taken into custody at the scene," Officer Sanchez says, "and she's been positively identified as the driver."

"What does she look like?" I ask.

As if he's just been waiting for me to ask, Officer Sanchez

yanks a large-screened phone from his breast pocket and taps a few keys. He zooms in, then hands me the phone. The screen is even brighter than the sun outside, or Officer Butler's star in the hospital that day. Even when I put on my shades, I still feel like I'm being stabbed in the eye with a thousand needles. But I can't look away.

What I'm looking at could be Gloria Carlton's mug shot. Even with the blinding glare, it looks sepia, like Gloria Carlton's skin. Gloria Carlton has short brown curls and freckles on both her cheeks. She has a moon-shaped face. Her eyes are droopy. She doesn't look like someone who would stand out in a crowd, someone you'd notice right away. She looks like someone who always wanted to be somewhere other than where she was. She looks like she's always tired.

"What did she say happened?" I hand Officer Sanchez back his phone.

"She claims it was an accident," Officer Sanchez says.

"You don't believe her?" I ask.

"Whenever we have a fatality, we have to investigate," Officer Butler chimes in.

"Are you sure you've never met her?" Dad asks me.

Every member of my family has their specialty. Grandpa Marcus and Grandma Régine's is organizing and planning things. Aunt Leslie's is medicine. Uncle Patrick's is music. Mom's is beauty, makeup, making people look good. Dad's is the law. Interviewing people and trying to better understand their stories is part of Dad's specialty.

"Did Izzie know this girl?" Dad asks.

"I don't know," I say. "I mean, I don't think so."

Maybe it was a mistake for me and Isabelle to try so hard to keep our school lives separate. Now there are questions I can't even answer about her. I wasn't with her all the time. I don't even know if some pyscho freshman wanted her dead.

"Where is she now?" I ask the officers.

"She's in her parents' custody," Officer Butler says.

"So she's out," I say.

"Yes," Officer Butler answers.

"Will I have to see her in school when I go back?" I ask.

"Her parents are using an online school," Officer Sanchez says.

"So nothing might happen to her," I say.

"We're still investigating," Officer Butler says. "We'll check in again and keep you up to date."

The interview is over. They wave goodbye and Josiane leads them to the door.

"Unbelievable," Dad says, after they leave.

Mom gets up and, with her arms still wrapped around her body, walks to the other side of the house. We can hear her sobbing just as clearly as if she were still sitting next to us. Aunt Leslie goes after her, and when she gets there, Mom's sobbing stops.

I am relieved when the doorbell rings again. This time it's Mrs. Clifton. Word must have gotten out that we were back from the service. The Marshalls also stop by with Pastor Ben. By then the house is so full, there's barely room for anyone to sit down.

Tina looks angrier than anything when I finally get to see her again. She fidgets while her parents greet mine, her five-foot frame shaking as she plops herself down on the sofa next to me.

"Let's go to your room," she says.

Turns out she'd come to rescue me. Tina is like my second sibling, my "untwinned" one, my *dosa*. You don't have to explain yourself to a *dosa*, either.

Going to my room, though, means walking past Isabelle's room. There's still that large handmade sign on her door that says STAY OUT! She made it after Mom got a note about drug abuse prevention from school and decided to regularly check our rooms.

I want to run rather than walk past the sign, but Tina puts her hand on the small of my back to hold me up, and I feel a little bit stronger.

My room is neater than I'd left it. The bed is all made and is lined up with the dresser whose drawers I'd left open with clothes spilling out that Friday evening. Josiane probably came through and tidied things up. Even my Jean Michel Brun portrait is already back on my wall.

I slip into my bed, pulling my clean pillows under my head. The pillows smell like a potpourri cushion. Tina walks to the other side of the bed and climbs in next to me. We're lying down, directly across from my print of Basquiat's *Riding with Death*.

Had Tina, Jean Michel, and I somehow known when we'd chosen it as one of our presentation prints that one day I would actually be riding with death?

I try to remember what we'd written about *Riding with Death*, what Tina had said in front of Mr. Rhys's class, that Basquiat must have known he was going to die young because in that painting he seemed to be so at ease with death. The man riding the skeleton seemed almost like he was on his way to a celebration, she said.

"How is our Jean Michel?" I ask Tina.

"He wanted to know if he could come see you later," she says.

I wonder where my phone is. In Mom's purse? In the wreckage of that car, probably with hundreds of messages on it.

Even though Gloria Carlton is the skeleton rider in our lives, I can't bring myself to talk about her right away. But maybe Tina knows her, so I have to ask.

"Do you know someone named—"

She interrupts me.

"The police came to the school," she says. "They talked to a bunch of us about her. Not that many people knew her."

"Why would she?" I couldn't even complete the thought. But why would Tina understand any of this better than I could?

"It might have been totally random," she says.

I know she doesn't mean to sound dismissive or casual about it, but she does. I know she's struggling with what to say, but why isn't she calling this Gloria person a murderer?

Suddenly I want her to go away. I want her to get off my bed, get out of my house, and just go away. I want everyone to go away. But if Tina goes away, I will lose yet another part of myself.

"Why didn't you come see me in the hospital?" I ask her.

"I did," she says, "though not for long."

"Really?"

"Your mom said we could only stay for thirty minutes."

"We?"

"Jean Michel and me."

"He came, too?"

"It was scary," she says. "Your eyes kept opening and closing, but it looked like you weren't there. Your were a medical mystery. Granddad called you Lazarus. Your aunt kept saying your stats looked good. She said that your brain scans looked fine, but you weren't waking up. From what they could tell, it didn't look like you were exactly in a coma. It just seemed like you were in a really deep sleep, except with your eyes open a lot of the time. You were like a horror-movie Sleeping Beauty."

That's exactly how I would have put it.

"When Jean Michel and I came to see you, we talked to you about school, especially art history and Rhys," she says. "He talked to you about that election campaign you guys worked on, and a bunch of other things. He was happy to see that portrait he made for you in your hospital room. Your grandma said she brought it there to remind you that you had family and friends who loved you."

"I kind of remember feeling some things," I say. "You told me stories to keep me alive."

"We tried," she says. "Seriously, though, we were really worried about you."

This is the most I've wanted to speak since the crash, and both the desire to say more and the act of trying tire me out. Still, it makes me realize how much I've missed Tina. I've missed how easy it is to talk to her.

"Did Jean Michel kiss me in the hospital?" I ask her.

"Basquiat?" she asks. "They must have given you some super-powerful drugs."

"You know what I mean."

"I sure do." She takes a deep breath and sighs to extend the torture.

"Well, did he?"

"He sure did." She sighs again. "I looked away to give you

guys some privacy, so I don't know if saliva was exchanged or anything."

I think I smile. Both now and way back there in the hospital, too.

"Let's get back to Gloria Carlton," I say anyway.

"Why?" she asks. "When we can talk forever about that kiss. Did you feel it?"

"I think I did."

"It must have been some kiss."

"I think it was."

I don't want to dilute the kiss with our words, and I really want to learn more about Gloria Carlton.

"Tell me everything," I say. "I know you must have Nancy Drewed her."

"I sure did," she says, switching now to co-detective mode. "There's nothing about Gloria Carlton online. No Facebook page. Nothing. It's like she doesn't exist."

I wish she didn't exist, I think, because then Isabelle would still be here.

"I hear voices," Aunt Leslie calls out from the other side of the door. "Can we come in?"

I want to ask who "we" is, but then she's already opened the door and she's standing there with Jean Michel Brun.

"Is everything all right in here?" Aunt Leslie asks.

She backs out of the room, leaving Jean Michel standing in the doorway.

"Come in," I say, and he does.

He looks around my room, as if taking everything in. My green curtains, the dimming light coming from the window, the posters on my wall, his portrait, the Basquiat print.

Tina gets up to make room for him on the bed, but then he motions for her to stay put and he squeezes himself between the two of us.

"Don't you guys have school today?" I ask.

"Today's Saturday," he says.

Grandma Régine brings us dinner in my room, large plates of sympathy food that could feed a small family: macaroni and cheese, fried chicken, a piece of pineapple upside-down cake, plus ice cream.

Comfort food galore, as Isabelle might say.

After we eat silently, Jean Michel carries our half-full plates out to the kitchen. He's gone for a while, so I guess he's either washing dishes or helping to load the dishwasher. Then I hear my parents talking to him about Gloria.

Dad's asking him if he knows her.

He doesn't know her, he says.

When Jean Michel comes back, Tina gets up to go to the bathroom.

"How are you holding up?" he asks me.

"I'm fine," I say, knowing how lame those words must sound given everything that's going on. Even the question is lame. He must know that, too.

"Everyone was so worried about you," he says.

"I heard."

"Shed a couple of tears when I was visiting you," he says.

"Nothing to be ashamed of," I say.

I don't want to dilute the kiss so I'm not going to ask. I'm not going to ask. I want to NOT ask, but I can't help myself.

"Did you kiss me in the hospital?" I ask him.

"I might have," he says, bobbing his head. "Was that bad?"

"No."

"Good," he says, his head still in motion. "I can help," he adds.

Help? How? By kissing me again? It's a nice thought, but I'm not sure he fully understands what he's saying. No one can really help. Not even him. Even though everyone thinks they can. By showing up. By bringing tons of food. By hugging me too tight.

"I can help," he says. "Tina, too. We're learning some great stuff in the computer science lab."

Then I finally catch on. He's telling me that he and Tina can help me learn more about Gloria Carlton. Maybe they have already learned more than Tina has let on. Knowing Tina, she probably wants me to be part of a big reveal.

"Thank you," I say.

"Call me," he says, "because I can't call you."

I wish he could touch my back again and make me forget myself. Make me forget everything.

"My phone," I say. "I don't know where my phone is."

Mom cracks the door open and puts her head through just as Tina's coming out of the bathroom.

Before I can ask Mom about the phone, she says, "Tina, your parents are leaving."

Mom tilts her head in Jean Michel's direction, making it clear that he has to go, too.

"I guess I'll see you soon," Jean Michel says.

"Sooner the better," Tina says.

When I was in the hospital and floating in and out of consciousness, I would have given anything to have my friends visit me. Had I known that they were there, I would have pleaded with them, begged them to stay. But now I'm kind of relieved to see them go.

I don't want to keep them trapped in this sad and lonely place with me. I want them to go out into the world with their fresh and hopeful eyes and never even have to think about my sister and me. I don't want them to be afraid that the next time they get into a car they might end up like her. Or that they might end up like me, riding this thing that I can't quite name. This thing that isn't really death, because it feels nothing like any other death I've been connected to. This thing that is partially like my own death. Or the death of this other girl I used to be.

The house is quiet after Jean Michel and Tina leave. Once the rest of the family goes to bed, I hear my parents talking in their bedroom across the hall. They're talking in low voices just like they used to, except they're not joking or talking about happy things. They're talking about Isabelle's funeral service.

They were sorry to have postponed it for so long, but they were glad that I was able to see Isabelle one last time. Wasn't it nice that so many people came? Maybe they shouldn't have called off the official repast Grandma Régine had planned for after the service. Nobody wanted that much fuss, though, even though it was hard to avoid. People came to the house anyway, Dad says.

They wonder how I'm holding up. Are they speaking to me enough? Even Aunt Leslie thinks I'm doing better than expected, Mom says. And what was wrong with those police officers, Dad asks? How come they can't figure out what's going on with that Carlton girl? And to just hand Giz that screen with the girl's face on it. How insensitive was that?

It's good that my friends came to spend a bit of time with me. They both agree on that. But too much time might not be so good, Mom says. They might make me go against the doctor's orders without meaning to, and keep me in front of screens all day long. Jean Michel seems like a nice boy, though, Dad says.

"Thank God for Tina," Mom says. "She always knows what Giz needs and when she needs it."

Mom and Dad are definitely a thing again.

According to Aunt Leslie, after Dad came home from the war, Mom asked him to come visit her in Miami. They hadn't seen each other since he'd joined the army.

Mom bought a special dress for the occasion, an off-the-shoulder red lace number. Dad was caught in traffic and was two hours late for their reunion dinner. Mom waited for him that whole time.

When he finally got to the restaurant, Dad sat down, put his head on Mom's shoulder, and asked, "When are we getting married?"

"Yesterday," she said.

They got married in front of a judge the next day.

That night, surprisingly, I hear a bit of laughter coming from my parents' bedroom.

Nothing can reunite fighting people more than a discussion of Grandma Régine's ways.

"Your mother *is* something else," Mom says.

"Who you telling?" Dad says.

I wait until I can't hear them anymore before heading into the shower.

Thanks to Josiane, or maybe it was Grandma Régine's handiwork, the bathroom shows no sign of Isabelle: no foggy mirrors, no sinks filled with soapy water, no wet towels draped over the bathtub, no robes or dirty underwear on the floor, nothing of hers in the cabinet except a strawberry-scented bodywash that she liked and I hated.

I pour the entire bottle over myself while sitting in the tub, letting the thick, sticky, strawberry-scented liquid slide down my back. I then hug the empty bottle tight and let the warm water wash it off of me.

The house is still quiet, so I throw on a T-shirt and shorts, then open the door to Isabelle's room. The light from the bathroom creates a path to her bed.

When we were little, we used to share a room, where we played indoor hopscotch and dared each other to see who could cannonball closest to the ceiling from our twin beds. We shared a flowered rug we called the Magic Carpet and a seashell chandelier that now hangs from Isabelle's ceiling. Her headboard is also a bookcase, where she mostly kept her acoustic speakers and magazines, some of which she'd had for years.

Across from her bed is a daybed that used to be her crib when she was a baby. (Mine is in storage somewhere.) On the daybed are two mason jars filled with dozens of buttons in different shapes, colors, and sizes. Some of the buttons are still in the tiny plastic bags in which they came, attached to the insides of brand-new clothes. One of those two jars had once been mine. I'd stopped collecting replacement—or understudy buttons, as she called them—but she hadn't. Everything else in her room, every wall, sheet, or curtain is either red, white, or black, her three favorite colors. She used her walls mostly as a bulletin board, for things she didn't want to forget. There's a large calendar above the daybed, with the day of the concert, the day of the car crash, circled in red. Next to the calendar are several pages of sheet music, some for the school orchestra, some for the church choir, and some that she was learning on her own.

Tacked to her reddest accent wall is a blown-up eight-by-ten-inch selfie of her and Ron Johnson on the beach with the two pilot whales in the background. Her cheek is pressed against Ron Johnson's cheek, and all their teeth are showing. She took that picture when they learned that the whales were going to be okay.

As I walk to her bed, I leave wet footprints on the cherry-wood floor, which would have driven her crazy. I look through her desk and skim through a few loose pages of her handwritten stories and poems, many of them with *To Be Put to Music One Day* printed in bold letters at the top.

Some of the pages have one word or two, which are written backwards as though to be read in a mirror. Words like love, heart, ron.

Is "ron" Ron?

Isabelle and I hadn't done any mirror writing since we were kids, leaving some of these same words, along with our names, as messages to each other on every mirror in the house.

I go through her closet and try on some of her clothes, her red skinny jeans, the ones with the holes at the knees, and two of her favorite T-shirts, with the faces of Scott Joplin—ragtime king—and Denyce Graves—opera goddess—printed on them. I put her crown of plastic red cardinal flowers on my head. We should have put it on her head, I think, in her coffin.

I try on her winter boots, the furry-looking brown ones she liked to wear to New York. And I even find some of my things in her closet, a hooded jumpsuit, a striped jersey dress, and a pair of sand-colored espadrilles.

This is a lot more than I should be doing. My neck is starting to feel wobbly, achy, not strong enough to hold my pulsating head. I stumble over to Isabelle's bed and climb under her red chenille throw and raise it over my head.

Slipping under her covers reminds me of when we were little girls and I used to jump into her bed. I would wake up from a nightmare and there she would be, waking up from the same nightmare, just in time to rock me back to sleep. Now I will always be alone with my nightmares.

The hallway door, the one with the STAY OUT sign, cracks open, and I hear footsteps. Someone is walking towards Izzie's bed. I hear a purr, from up high, not from the floor. Dessalines is in somebody's arms.

When I pull the throw off my head, I see Mom and Dad there. Dad is leaning on his crutches in the doorway. Half his body is broken. He's wearing a tank top and pajama shorts. Mom is standing next to the bed in one of her long nightgowns. She's holding Dessalines.

"I thought I heard someone in here," Dad says from the doorway.

"Didn't mean to scare you guys," I say.

"I think we scared each other," Mom says.

"It's been strange having both rooms empty while you were still in the hospital," Dad says. His words fall so heavy on all of us that if we were a ship at sea, they'd immediately sink us to the bottom.

My parents seem to realize that there are no safe places left in the super-booby-trapped minefield all around us, so they stand there quietly, both of them staring at me, until Dessalines's purring momentarily snaps us all out of it.

"Thought you might like some company," Mom says.

She leans over and puts Dessalines in my arms. Dessalines

rubs his whiskers against my cheeks. He starts kneading my chest with his paws, then slips away and curls up at the foot of the bed.

Dad wobbles over on his crutches, and Mom helps him slide onto one side of the bed. He groans as if in agony while sitting on Isabelle's super-hard mattress. Mom turns off the light and climbs in on the other side of me. They are guarding me like rails, as if to keep me from falling.

The bed creaks under all our weight, and I'm afraid that the box spring might snap and come crashing down, but it doesn't.

Dessalines dashes off.

"I don't think that cat likes any of us," Dad says.

"I think he just liked Izzie," Mom says.

I'm tempted to say, "Remember when . . ." and tell some story about Izzie and Dessalines. There are so many.

"Remember when Izzie accidently dropped Dessalines in the pool, then dived in to save him and he nearly scratched her eyes out?" I say.

"I don't think it was an accident," Dad says. "I think she was trying to see if he could swim."

"We learned that day that cats don't like water," Mom says.

"That bugger sure can swim, though," Dad says.

"They made up right afterwards," Mom says. "Which proves my theory. I don't think he would have forgiven any of us the way he forgave her."

Izzie's bed was the only one Dessalines would ever sleep in.

Another "Remember when" moment.

When Dessalines first came to live with us, I had a cold that my parents thought was a cat allergy, and we almost gave Dessalines away.

"Can we give Giz away instead?" Izzie asked my parents.

Once, when he came to Sunday dinner with his latest girl-friend, Dad's friend Moy told Dad that we were dishonoring the name of the great Haitian revolutionary Jean-Jacques Dessalines by giving it to a cat.

I couldn't tell whether my parents were mortified or proud when Isabelle took it upon herself to offer a monologue as rebuttal.

"Isn't it great to honor the things and people we love in what-ever way we can, to keep them as close to us as possible, in both body and mind? Isn't it better to call a cat Dessalines than to forget Dessalines? At least here, we call out Dessalines's name several times a day. Aren't there people who call their chil-dren Dessalines? Yes, I know you'll want to tell me that a cat is not the same as a child. What if the cat is my child? And are you absolutely sure that there are no cats whatsoever in all of the United States of America that are named after George Washington or Abraham Lincoln or Thomas Jefferson? If not, we should change that."

She was channeling her two-year winning streak in debate team, but I think she was mostly trying to impress Moy's TV newscaster girlfriend, who was a new audience for her.

I don't remember the rest of the speech, but I thought I heard a rousing rendition of "Battle Hymn of the Republic" playing in the background as she brought it to a close. I half expected her to get up on the table, fist raised while waiting for her standing ovation.

"She'll make a great politician one day," Moy said.

Mom and Dad just shook their heads.

"I think she's already one now," Moy's girlfriend said.

But student government and the like never interested her. They required too much time—much like the debate team had—time that she wanted to devote to her music. The thing about it being okay to call a cat Dessalines was yet another thing she wanted to put to music one day.

My parents and I share all this, with what exact words I'm not sure. The words drift between us, and we each take turns filling in some of the gaps. Until we fall asleep.

CHAPTER 24

UNCLE PATRICK AND Alejandra leave for New York the next day. Aunt Leslie is going to hang around a while longer, and it seems like Grandma Régine and Grandpa Marcus will be staying until the beginning of the summer.

Grandpa Marcus and Aunt Leslie drive Mom and Dad to their doctors' appointments and I stay with Grandma Régine. Not being able to read, write, sketch or draw, look at screens, or see my friends, the only thing left to do is listen to the radio.

I search up and down the dial on the kitchen radio to find a local news station that mentions us, but none of them do. I am thinking we're already yesterday's news, or no news at all, when Grandma Régine, after finding a Creole station that's broadcasting news from Haiti, hands me a folder full of newspaper clippings.

Sometimes Grandma Régine is an actual rebel, even if a silent one. Here she is, handing me newspaper articles when I'm not even allowed to have visitors who might show me words.

Mom told Tina and Jean Michel Brun to stay away until the doctor cleared me for screens. It doesn't seem fair that people were allowed to come and see me when I was in the hospital, but not at home. Thankfully, Grandma Régine is not a full-on believer in absolute medical decrees.

The words in Grandma Régine's newspaper clippings blur into black masses, but I can make out the pictures if I look away now and then. Or after I close then reopen my eyes.

The first article must be about the crash because there's a picture of the wrecked cars, both ours and the one Gloria Carlton was driving. It's strange to see the aftermath the way others have seen it. The cars are not as mashed together as I would have thought. The front of the red minivan is mostly gone, but our car is pretty much whole except on Izzie's side, which is caved in. Even Dad's door was spared in comparison. Izzie did take the brunt of it, for all of us.

The next article has our recent school portraits, mine and Isabelle's. I can tell that the pictures were downloaded from our school photographer's website because his name stamp is still on them. The third article is about Isabelle's death. It's the front page of the *Miami Herald*. The headline is so big that I can easily make it out. TEEN TWIN CAR CRASH VICTIM DIES.

I squint to see what they wrote about Isabelle, but I see my name where Isabelle's should be. I am the one everyone thought had died.

I imagine Ron Johnson and all of Isabelle's friends seeing the story and thinking Isabelle is alive, then finding out she's dead, their guilty disappointment that it wasn't me who'd died.

The next clipping explains the mistake, or so it seems, from the few lines I can make out before my head starts throbbing again.

When the Haitian news program is over, Grandma Régine asks me if I want her to read any of the articles to me.

I shake my head no. Even though I know this is a big thing coming from her. She doesn't like reading to people, and she doesn't like reading in English. So basically she's trying to do me a solid, as Dad might say.

"You don't have to read it to me," I say. "I know how it turns out."

Except I don't.

Once my head stops throbbing, I look again through the pile of newspaper clippings that Grandma Régine has so carefully cut out for me. Knowing her, she probably did it in case I got amnesia or something.

When I look again through the pile, I concentrate on Gloria Carlton. The picture Officer Sanchez showed me is above one of the articles. There's also a picture of Gloria Carlton and her parents leaving the police station. She has a sweatshirt draped over her head, and her parents are holding her elbows, guiding her towards a waiting car.

Something about the picture seems odd to me, but I can't immediately figure it out. After all, there's nothing more common than people walking out of police stations with their faces covered. Who would want to be seen after what Gloria Carlton had done?

I keep having to close and reopen my eyes to avoid the jabbing pain in them, but each time I look at the picture of Gloria and her parents leaving the police station, it still feels like I am looking at it for the first time.

Is my short-term memory loss finally kicking in? Have I pushed my eyes, my brain too far?

Something tells me to look at the picture again, and this time I see what's catching my attention. Gloria Carlton's father is digging his fingernails into her bare elbow. He is biting down on his lower lip and is frowning so hard that his bushy eyebrows meet in the middle of his forehead.

Gloria's mother has a fixed, nervous smile on her face. She's pulling Gloria forward with one hand while waving the photographers away with the other. There's a large gap between the three of them, as though the mother is trying to run away from both Gloria and her father.

I ask Grandma Régine to read the tiny caption for me. She reads, "Teen emerges from police station after spending night in custody."

Just then we hear a key in the door. Grandma Régine quickly grabs the folder from me.

Dad's crutches hit the floor like tap shoes as he makes his way to the couch. Mom is looking a lot better than him. She now has a series of pretty knit berets that she uses to cover her ever-shrinking bandages.

"What have you been up to?" Mom asks.

They're back to echoing each other's sentences, so Dad adds, "Yeah, what have you been doing with yourselves?"

Grandma Régine and I look at each other.

"Not much," Grandma Régine says.

We nod to each other conspiratorially.

That night I search Isabelle's room for some clues about whether or not she'd known Gloria Carlton. There are no hidden diaries in her drawers, no secret letters in her closet. Everything I hadn't already seen would either be on her laptop or cell phone.

I look around her room for her school backpack, but it's nowhere to be found. Maybe the police have it. Or maybe Mom and Dad do. They wouldn't give me the phones anyway. Tina will have to help me.

I use the house phone and call Tina while sitting on the kitchen floor in the dark. The call goes to voice mail. Tina's probably asleep.

As much as I try, I can't remember Jean Michel's cell number. I try a few guesses and end up getting wrong numbers.

I'm tempted to go to Mom's home office and use her computer, but I'm afraid that the light will be so blinding that I won't get anywhere at all.

"I'm not going to turn on the light," I hear a voice say. "I'm just going to slide down here next to you."

It's Aunt Leslie.

She opens the freezer side of the refrigerator and pulls out a pint of ice cream, then sits down on the floor beside me. We pass around the little plastic spoon that comes with the ice cream and we gobble up all three flavors of the Neapolitan until the container is empty.

"You have to follow the doctor's instructions," she says. "You have to comply. And that's the doctor and not your aunt talking."

"It's hard to just stay in the house and do nothing," I say.

"Was it better in the hospital?"

"I'll try to do better."

"You better do better," she says and chuckles.

"Thank you for hanging out with us so long," I say.

"That's what family's for," she says, "to torture you and to love you and sometimes both at the same time."

I remember a few months back when Mom, Dad, Isabelle, and I went to spend a weekend at her house in Orlando. She and Mom disappeared for hours without telling any of us where they went. We thought they were planning something big, a surprise for Dad, or for all of us. Now I realize they might have been discussing Mom and Dad's separation.

Because Aunt Leslie always likes it when you get right to the point, I tell her, "I miss Izzie so much."

"I know," she says. "Me, too."

"You think that girl was trying to hurt Izzie?" I ask.

"I don't know," she says.

"Maybe she hated her or was jealous of her."

"Nobody could hate your sister," she says.

Because we loved Izzie so much, we couldn't imagine anyone not loving her, too.

"I need Izzie's phone," I say.

"The police have your phones," she says.

"Izzie has a backup contact list online. Maybe this girl's number's on Izzie's contact list."

"Do you know Izzie's password?" she asks.

"No."

"I thought twins were supposed to be able to read each other's minds."

"Sometimes, but not all the time."

"There's a lot I'm learning about you two," she says.

"Could you really not tell us apart?" I ask.

"What makes you say that?"

I want to tell her that I heard everything while I was under, but I know it would lead to her asking me all kinds of medical questions, so I don't.

"You two did have me fooled sometimes," she says.

"If we could find Izzie's laptop," I say.

"The police have that, too," she says. "They also have both your book bags."

"So they're thinking this girl and Izzie might have known each other?"

"It also could have been an accident," she says. "But they want to be sure.

"We can try a few guesses for Izzie's password to get her contact list," she adds. "But tomorrow. Not tonight."

"Why not tonight?"

"We're not going to do anything else tonight but go back to bed."

"Ever the doctor," I say.

"That's one of your mother's favorite things to say to me."

"I know.

"Mom's proud of you," I add. "She's always said that, too."

"Well, I'm proud of her for having raised such amazing daughters. I must remind you, though, oh you amazing daughter, that part of your recovery is resting and not working yourself up into a state like you did just now."

"I'm not in a state," I say. "I'm calm." Though that's not really true. I'm more frustrated than anything else, by how little I'm able to do, both for my sister and for myself.

"You know what's going on with your parents—I mean their separation talk—you know that has nothing to do with you, right?" she says, changing the subject.

"I'm not five years old," I say.

I know she understands why I'm snapping at her. I need someone to tell when nothing makes sense to me, and the person I'd be telling, my sister, is gone.

"I know you're not five years old," she says. "I'm only letting you know that this is their MO."

"Their MO?"

"Their modus operandi. Their mode of operation. Your parents often try to separate, like when he left Haiti, or when he went to the army, or for a couple of weeks when you and Izzie were too young to remember. Then they realize that they can't live without each other. They write each other a bunch of sappy letters. I bet they write emails these days, which is too bad because I won't have access to them. Then at some point they get back together. Your dad works less. Your mom finds another purpose in life. And all is well again. Then a few years later, it happens again. It's so exhausting to watch. I think that's why I'm not married."

This is the best news I've heard in a while.

"You promise?" I ask.

"I can't make any promises," she says. "But I know them and I'd put some good money on it. Though you have to give them time. There's losing your sister now. But even before everything they've just been through, your mom was already struggling with becoming a wife and mother so early in her life."

There were no letters about any of this in Mom and Dad's box of letters. I never thought of Isabelle's and my being born as having stopped Mom's life in any way. But I guess it must have. Having a husband in school and two babies at home, all in her early twenties, couldn't have been easy.

Dad was going to law school for the first couple of years of our lives, Aunt Leslie says. And since Dad's law specialty is not the most profitable one he could have chosen, Grandpa Marcus had to buy them this house. Once we were in school, Mom did the occasional odd job, which is how she learned to do makeup.

"I didn't know any of this," I say.

"Parents try to protect their children from a lot of things," she says, "including their own failures and heartbreak."

"What did she want to do?" I ask.

"She used to want to be a teacher."

"She can still do that."

"Then a pilot. Then an engineer. She's not sure."

"Maybe they're splitting up for real this time, then—"

"So she can do all those things?"

"Or one of them."

"Your parents may not realize this themselves," she says, "but they love each other in this first love kind of way, and I think they're afraid that it will become this friendship kind of thing, so the drama continues."

It was strange to think of my parents as these lost souls who were trying to live out some all-consuming love affair in boring everyday life.

"This is all between us, of course," Aunt Leslie says.

"Of course," I say.

"With all secrets out of the way, I can now be your sidekick," she says.

"You promise?"

"Pinkie promise."

We linked pinkies in the dark.

"We'll look up the stuff you need after your doctor's visit," she says. "Your folks asked me to take you."

I had completely forgotten about the doctor's visit. Maybe I tried to block it out.

"I'm so over doctors," I say, "except you."

"I'm glad you said except me," she says, "because I'm thinking of leaving the practice in Orlando and joining one in Miami. Your mom and I discussed it even before all this happened."

"For real?" I want to shriek with joy, but then I realize why she's moving in the first place. It's probably to look after Mom, which means that in spite of their MO, my parents might really end things this time.

"I'll be sad to leave my patients," she says, "but it will be great to be near all of you."

She wraps her arms around my shoulder, and more than hugging her back, I try to disappear into her.

"No one will ever replace Izzie in your life," she says. "We're not even going to try. But we still want to be here for you."

Of all the odd things that people—and by people I mean people like Aunt Leslie's friend Dr. Aidoo—always want to tell twins, one is that there are tons of seemingly untwinned people who have been carrying some version of their unborn twins inside of them their whole lives. It's called fetus in fetu. Some of these people are fetus-in-fetu marked, or have dark or hairy birthmarks to show for it, a micro-silhouette of their lost sibling. Others are walking around with parts of their twins inside of them, tiny lungs and spinal cords and even teeth.

I have never liked fetus in fetu. I want twins that you can see, walking around. Alive.

But what are you called when your twin dies?

I want some name other than twinless twin. I want something simple, lyrical, sophisticated sounding. Even though I know it would never fully comfort me, I want something beautiful to now call myself.

If we were Yoruba, because she came out first, Isabelle would have been Taiwo, or the one who first took in the world. I would have been Kehinde, the one who followed. Now that

Isabelle is gone, someone would have carved a small statue of her, an effigy for me to keep with me at all times.

"Can I still call myself a twin?" I ask Aunt Leslie.

She seems stumped. According to Dr. Aidoo, some people think that twins share a single soul. If this is true, then where is my soul now?

"I imagine you'll be a twin forever," Aunt Leslie says.

She reaches for Isabelle's necklace, which is hanging around her neck, and holds the Hand of Fatima pendant in the palm of her hand.

"Your mother said I could wear this until you wanted it," she says.

Before I can say anything, she takes the necklace off and puts it around my neck.

Now I am wearing both.

"Believe it or not," she says while stroking her neck where the necklace was, "one day you'll be able to think of her, smile, tell jokes, and laugh."

"That's hard to imagine right now," I say.

"Sometimes it comes even sooner than you expect," she says.

"How do you know all of this?" I ask.

"Not all my patients grow up," she says.

I never thought of that.

"I often have to think of what to say to their parents and siblings," she says.

"What's the best thing you've ever said?"

"It depends on the parent. The child. The sibling."

"What would you say to me?"

"What would I say?"

She rubs her chin for effect.

"Apparently, in many places in the universe, when one twin dies, the gods turn the other one's sadness into stars."

This is a kind of thing that Isabelle might have loved hearing about, that we might have loved hearing about together.

"Is that all you got?" I ask, teasing Aunt Leslie.

"I'm afraid it is," she says.

"What if I don't have those types of godly connections?" I ask her.

"You mean you don't know any gods that can hook you up?" she says.

"You did not just say 'hook up.'"

"My bad," she says.

"You did not just say 'my bad,' either."

"Guilty as charged," she says.

"Do you talk to your patients this way?"

"I try to stay au courant, yes."

She laughs and I'm surprised how easy that laughter comes, how easy laughter has always come to people in our family, even when we are arguing, or fighting, or even mourning. I love sitting on the kitchen floor, eating ice cream and giggling with my aunt, the way she, Isabelle, and I have done so many times before, while talking about schools, boys, and even while complaining about our parents.

"Do you want to speak to someone on a regular basis?" she asks.

"I'm speaking to you," I say.

"I mean a social worker. Counselor?"

"I'm talking to you," I repeat.

"I failed you," she says.

"Why would you say that?"

"In the hospital that day, I shouldn't have let you know that Isabelle died. I wasn't planning to. I just wanted you to wake up so bad. I messed up."

"I needed to know," I say. "So that thing with the gods and the stars could start happening."

I think now that I might have felt the moment Isabelle died.

It was most likely when Officer Butler's badge exploded in my head, when those red and auburn stars burst before my eyes. The beeps and alarms must have been for Isabelle and not me. Everyone must have been racing to save her. The feeling of lightning hitting my chest must have been from the resuscitation paddles they'd used to try to restart her heart. And when that final beep faded, Isabelle must have taken her last breath. Then she must have pulled me under, carrying me away with her for a while.

CHAPTER 25

I AM BEGINNING to lose track of the school-related flow of time, but I know that it's the last day of school before Easter break.

"Are you still quarantined?" Tina calls on the house phone to ask. "Whenever Jean Michel and I call, your mom says you can't talk. I can't wait for you to have your phone back."

At breakfast, Mom and Dad seem worried when I ask if Tina and Jean Michel can come over and visit me. It's as if suddenly everyone is suspect. Everyone can hurt me.

Ever the mediator, Aunt Leslie asks if, after taking me to see Dr. Aidoo, she can take me to visit my school. That way I can see my friends there, even for a little while.

"I don't see how that's going to help," Mom says.

"Who's the doctor here?" Aunt Leslie asks.

"It will do her some good," Dad agrees.

Grandpa Marcus tries to distract us by spreading out the plans for his cathedral in the middle of the breakfast table. Construction is set to begin in the summer. Grandpa Marcus had been working on some adjustments early that morning. The plans are too large and much too detailed for any of us to understand.

"Why don't you make 3-D versions of these plans?" I tell Grandpa Marcus.

"I've been waiting for it," Dad says. "I've been waiting for it."

"What?" Mom asks.

"What Giz just said. This is exactly what Izzie would have said at this very moment."

I walk over, wrap my arms around Mom's shoulder, then Dad's good side, and I squeeze them both as hard as I can manage and as hard as they can take. They both seem surprised, but reach back and hold me even tighter. This is my way of thanking them for Isabelle and me, for everything they had to give up because of us.

Dr. Aidoo greets me like an old friend, a really old friend.

He gets up from behind his desk to pull out a chair for me. He and Aunt Leslie do small talk, during which I learn from her asking about his mother and father in Accra that he is from

Ghana. I also learn that he has an ex-wife. The *ex* part seems to make Aunt Leslie smile.

I gather from the much sadder strands of the conversation that Dr. Aidoo had seen Isabelle when they first brought her into the hospital, when she was put on a respirator.

Dr. Aidoo and Aunt Leslie reaffirm that they must stay in very close touch—and he nearly drags the word *touch* into a sentence—about my case.

I think they see me rolling my eyes, so they start talking shop. Almost.

It seems that Aunt Leslie had indeed known him before, in medical school, and knowing that he had privileges in our hospital, among others, she had specifically requested him for my and Isabelle's case.

They then travel down some censored version of medical school memory lane, which includes a few tales of binge drinking, and some other things they were trying to keep from me by speaking about them in medical code. This goes on and on even while he listens to my heart and listens to me breathe, looks into my ears, looks into my eyes, looks into Aunt Leslie's eyes, then checks how long I can follow his fingers back and forth, and hold my arm out, and how many times I can walk around his tiny office that way.

When we're done, he tells me that he could consider letting me go back to school in a few weeks after he's taken a new MRI.

He also agrees with Aunt Leslie that it's okay for me to visit my school that day. I think he would say yes to nearly anything Aunt Leslie suggests.

I feel bad for all the times I thought of him as a big duck. He probably would have scolded me for writing him a thank-you letter, so I just come out and say it again: "Thank you very much."

"I'm glad Leslie called me," he says, keeping his eyes on her face.

They kiss each other goodbye on both cheeks, in this kind of awkward way people do when they're trying real hard for their lips not to meet.

I roll my eyes again and he says, "See, even your eye rotations are getting stronger."

After we leave Dr. Aidoo's office, I wait until Aunt Leslie starts the car before I ask about their past. I had not hallucinated him at the funeral home that day. He had actually been there.

I close my eyes so I don't have to see the road, then I say, "You totally used to hit that, didn't you?"

She pretends not to hear me. Then I open my eyes for a second and look over at her, and I see a little smirk growing wider and wider across her face.

I hate to admit it, but she and the head duck would probably make a cute brainy couple.

"Well, you can say that he and I both used to hit it," she says.

"Is he the one that got away?" I ask.

"How do you know such things?"

"Hello, I live in the world. And I watch romantic comedies. Or I used to."

"Then there is a silver lining to your current condition," she says.

"Are you going to do something about this?" I ask.

"About what?"

"About Dr. Duck?"

"What did you call him?"

"I mean Dr. Aidoo."

"Why do I have to do something about it?" she asks. "Is that the rule in your romantic comedies?"

"Is he doing something about it?"

"Maybe," she says, her eyes beaming in a way that would have probably blinded me if I weren't wearing my cat eyes.

"We're going to try to find some way to work together," she says. "Maybe I'll join his practice here."

"How sexy," I say.

Here is Aunt Leslie taking a big leap with Dr. Duck, while my parents are about to let go.

"I haven't told anyone yet," she says. "You're the first person I'm telling, besides him, of course."

Maybe to keep me quiet, Aunt Leslie drives me right to Morrison. When we get to the school, before we go anywhere, Principal Volcy wants to meet with Aunt Leslie and me.

This has been arranged by Aunt Leslie and my parents, I realize when I end up sitting in front of the principal's desk with Aunt Leslie in the next seat.

"We've already had an assembly to talk about your sister," Principal Volcy tells me.

Thank goodness they've already done it, I think, because I can't imagine sitting through one of those.

"We also had grief counselors, and many of the kids have taken advantage of those," she says.

Has Gloria Carlton taken advantage of the grief counselors, I want to ask, but don't.

"Again, I'm so very sorry," Principal Volcy says. "We're cooperating fully with the police in whatever way we can."

"What did the police want to know from you?" Aunt Leslie asks her.

"I'm sure they would tell you themselves," Principal Volcy says.

"We just want to get some idea from you," Aunt Leslie says.

Aunt Leslie is a great sidekick even though we couldn't figure out Isabelle's password, which I bet Isabelle did her best to keep secret from me. She hadn't chosen any of the obvious choices. Or at least the ones that seemed obvious to me. The ones I have, or would have chosen myself. She did not choose her middle name or my name or Dessalines's name; Ron Johnson or pilot whales or any titles or famous lines or abbreviations of famous lines from the books and movies we loved. I bet Tina and Jean Michel can hack into Isabelle's account, but I'm not ready to ask them yet.

"Well." Principal Volcy pauses and looks me over carefully. "The detectives served us a warrant for Gloria's school records. They want to make sure what happened was actually an accident, that she wasn't purposefully targeting anyone."

I give Aunt Leslie an "I told you so" look as we head out of Principal Volcy's office.

Part of me hopes that I will run into Isabelle in the halls, just as I did sometimes when I was least expecting it. She would catch me daydreaming or doing a WWR (Walking While Reading) and bump into me on purpose.

"Hey, Giz," she'd call out. "Wake up!"

Aunt Leslie and I get out of Principal Volcy's office just in time to make French class.

Walking the school hallway, even with Aunt Leslie next to me, I feel like every inch of the school is haunted. People, students, staff, even the janitors, can't help but stare at me. Kids I've never seen before wave to me and I wave back, in part with gratitude. At least they can see me. At least I'm here.

Thank goodness Aunt Leslie is with me, to help me get through some of the quick hugs, the overfriendliness of strangers, the too loud "That's her" that people think I can't hear. Since I'm wearing my cat-eyed glasses inside, maybe some are wondering if I'm now blind. Others whisper Isabelle's name as they walk past me. The same kind of confusion that might have happened when Isabelle was alive is happening still. They're not sure who they're looking at. Or maybe they're asking themselves the same question I am. Why her and why not me?

Aunt Leslie drops me off at the door of French class. She wants to go in with me, but I don't let her. I take a deep breath and walk inside.

Everyone is already seated. I take the seat closest to the door, hoping that both the class and Madame Blaise will act as if nothing is different from the last time I was there.

Madame Blaise's going on as though I'm not even there makes me think they've been rehearsing for my return.

Just act normal, she might have told them.

Still, there are whispers, and notes are being passed. I don't even have a notebook to doodle in. Madame Blaise walks over, leans down, and whispers, "*Je suis désolée.*"

I get up and leave.

Aunt Leslie and I go and sit in the empty school auditorium for a while.

My head fills up with images of past gatherings there: pep rallies, award ceremonies, talent shows, speaker days, career days, holiday pageants, all things that Isabelle and I attended together, even while sitting in different parts of the auditorium with our own sets of friends.

This is where the spring orchestra concert was supposed to take place. This is where it had taken place last year and the year before that. When no one had died.

The black curtains were supposed to part and Isabelle was supposed to be sitting up there on the stage playing Stravinsky with her friends. We were supposed to arrive early and find seats near the front row. We were not supposed to be late. We weren't supposed to not be there at all.

Aunt Leslie agrees to let me try one more class visit.

What a strange experiment we've undertaken. Yet spending another day at home resting might have been harder still.

In art history, Mr. Rhys changes his lesson plan as soon as I walk through the door. I can tell because everyone is shuffling pages, trying to find what he's talking about.

He's going to talk briefly about grief art, he announces.

The idea was just to say hi to Mr. Rhys and maybe pick up a few reading assignments I could do when I was feeling better, then leave. But then he asks if I'll stick around for a few minutes. Maybe this is why I also want to be here, to be part of some kind of reassuring performance for my friends, live grief art.

Jean Michel turns around and looks at me and just about everyone else does, too, except Tina, who keeps her head down.

Mr. Rhys has to use the Smart Board to quickly find some good examples of paintings that show the five stages of grief. He dims the lights and logs in. The names of the five stages of grief pop up neatly on the board.

1. *Denial and Isolation*
2. *Anger*
3. *Bargaining*
4. *Depression*
5. *Acceptance*

"On now to finding the art to match them," Mr. Rhys says.

I can still feel everyone looking at me. The screen is so bright it seems like it's sending daggers into my eyeballs. I feel a new kind of pain, like a hammer repeatedly landing on my forehead.

I close my eyes to avoid the grinding pain. I stagger over to my empty seat next to Tina and Jean Michel. Jean Michel reaches over and takes my hand. His hands are as sweaty as mine. He's nervous for me, I think, about what might show up on that screen.

If I were Mr. Rhys, I'd choose a different painting for every grief milestone he's listed. For Denial and Isolation, I'd show Frida Kahlo's *The Two Fridas* (*Las Dos Fridas*), in which Frida Kahlo is holding hands with a mirror image of herself, their two exposed hearts joined by one vein. For Anger, I'd show Edvard Munch's swirly ghost in *The Scream*. For Bargaining ("If we'd left fifteen minutes earlier . . ."), I'd show one of Isabelle's favorite Haitian artists, Louisiane Saint Fleurant's portraits of bubble-headed twins. For Depression, I'd show Alison Saar's *Barefoot*, a life-size wood sculpture of a woman coiled into a fetal position, weeping as a tree grows from the soles of her feet. And for Acceptance, I'd show Basquiat's *Riding with Death*.

I don't know what Mr. Rhys actually shows. I'm not sticking around to find out. I pull my hand away from Jean Michel's and walk out. As I'm rushing away, my arm grazes the back of Jean Michel's neck and I nearly lose my balance.

I wish I had given myself more time. I am trying to fast-forward my life so I can put more distance between that awful night and me. I want to figure out how people can go on with their lives when mine has changed so much. I want to relearn how to breathe without carrying this big, empty cave inside me.

Tina and Jean Michel rush out behind me. Aunt Leslie is waiting right outside the door.

"We'll go with you," Tina says.

I don't want them with me. I am jealous of them. I'm jealous of them because they can read and watch a screen. I'm jealous because they can look at a newspaper without getting a headache. I'm jealous because they still think French and art history classes matter.

"It's okay. I got this," Aunt Leslie says. "You two go back to class."

They hesitate, then together step back into the classroom. I can tell that Tina wants me to send Jean Michel away and ask her to stay with me. My asking them both to leave me alone is like putting my lifelong friendship with her on the same fragile ground as whatever possibly romantic thing might be happening between Jean Michel and me.

Before I walk away, I see Tina looking through the Plexiglas panel in the door, and I know that she's feeling both worried and betrayed. But there's not much I can do for her. There's not much I can even do for myself. Every kind of comfort either she or Jean Michel could offer me would only keep reminding me of everything that was now impossible for Isabelle, everything that she would never experience, everything that she would never feel, everything that she would never know.

Jean Michel squeezes his face in next to Tina's in the small square opening. Their eyes, mouths, chins now block out everything I once loved and am leaving behind: those slides and screenshots, those paintings, Mr. Rhys, the two of them. Alone. Together. Without me.

CHAPTER 26

THE NEXT DAY I get a visit from Ron Johnson. Aunt Leslie and Grandpa Marcus are dropping Mom and Dad off at their respective doctors. I'm home with Grandma Régine and we're sitting on the couch listening to a call-in Haitian news program. The doorbell rings. Grandma Régine walks over, opens the front door, and Ron Johnson is standing there holding a massive bouquet of white roses.

Grandma Régine thinks he's selling the individual flowers, so she leaves the door half-open and asks him to wait while she gets her purse. He doesn't quite hear or understand her, so he follows her inside.

I nearly jump out of my skin when I see him. He seems startled, too, as though in all the versions of storming Isabelle's castle that he's imagined, none of them were so easy.

Grandma Régine has already picked up her purse and is searching for the money when she looks up and sees Ron Johnson handing the sympathy bouquet to me.

"How much?" she asks anyway.

Ron Johnson is confused. He looks at me, then at Grandma Régine, then finally says, "They're a gift for your family. They're not for sale."

"Oh," Grandma Régine says.

She puts her purse down and walks over with one of the many vases we've accumulated from the endless flower deliveries after Isabelle died.

I am so speechless that I forget to tell Ron Johnson to sit down. So Grandma Régine tells him to. She puts the flowers on the coffee table, making it a much-needed island between Ron and me. She then walks to the front door and closes it, all while keeping an eye on us.

Ron says nothing and I don't say anything, either. Short of asking him why he's here, I can't think of anything to say.

"You're the boy from the wall?" Grandma Régine finally recognizes him.

"The wall?" Ron asks.

"Isabelle's wall," Grandma Régine says.

"Isabelle has a picture of you in her room," I say.

"A rather large one," Grandma Régine says. "Of the two of you together."

Ron Johnson seems both flattered and surprised, as though this was the last thing he was expecting to hear.

I imagine Isabelle being mortified by Grandma Régine's blabbing. Grandma Régine has just given away a secret that Isabelle might not have wanted Ron Johnson to know. But what does it matter anyway? The dead are not allowed secrets.

"Would you like something to drink?" Grandma Régine asks Ron.

"Maybe some water," he says. "Please."

While Grandma Régine is getting the water, Ron Johnson says, "Her accent is pretty."

"So many people in my life have accents. I don't even hear them anymore," I say.

"I guess that can happen," he says.

I want to ask him how he got our address, but it's so easy to get anybody's address, anybody's but Gloria Carlton's.

I wonder if he knew her, so I ask him.

He quickly says, "No," as though he would never want to know her or anyone remotely like her.

"I haven't seen you at school," he says.

I want to ask him if he ever saw me before, with or without Isabelle. I guess he must have. If he was in class with Isabelle or was interested in her, he must have at least heard about me.

"I'm not back yet," I say. "Doctor says I need to rest." As in hint hint, maybe you're keeping me from resting.

Grandma Régine brings him a glass of water so frosty that the glass is sweating. She brings one for me, too, because she considers it rude to let people drink alone in your house, even if they're only drinking water. If you don't drink with them, they might think you're poisoning them, she says.

My glass is so cold that it is making my fingertips feel numb. I take a sip, then place the glass on the coaster she hands me with it. Ron pushes his head back and drinks the whole thing in a couple of gulps. Grandma Régine takes the glass and coaster from him, still watching him carefully as she walks away.

"I guess you must be wondering why I'm here." He makes his voice purposely deep to sound like the man he might become in a few years.

I know why he's here. He finds it hard to say goodbye to Isabelle, and he thinks he can keep saying it to me. But I can't be a grave site for him to visit and bring flowers to. I can't become a living memorial for him. I also can't expand Isabelle for him, give him any more of her than he's already had.

Isabelle is now finite. I can't give any more of her away. So if she hadn't told him what her favorite fruit was or what her favorite colors were or what she dreamed about most often, tough luck. He should just keep what he has, without carving into mine. But sometimes not knowing some things, even one thing, makes it harder to say goodbye.

"So Isabelle told you about the whales," he says.

"She did."

"Did she tell you anything else?"

I tell him that she didn't, which is true.

"You know what she kept saying that day with the whales?"

"No."

"What were you doing that day?" he asks.

I try to think back. Then it comes to me. I was doing what everyone in my year was doing, everyone except him and Isabelle. I was taking a mock SAT test.

"That whole day," he says, "she kept saying"—He takes a stab at mimicking Isabelle's voice, my voice, which isn't bad at all. He has the quavering tone and pitch just right.—"'I wish my sister could see this. Wait until I tell my sister about this.' She would have called you except she didn't want to mess up your test."

I feel a knot growing in my throat and tears gathering in my eyes. Ron Johnson has actually come to give me something, rather than take something from me. He understands that when you lose someone, it's as if they've been smashed into a thousand pieces and what you're doing in the aftermath is gathering a few of those pieces to put some version of that person back together again. And not all of the pieces are yours. Some of them belong to other people. Part of Isabelle now belongs to Ron Johnson, too.

"Can I please see her room?" he asks.

I realize now that this is why he came here in the first place. He and Isabelle might have planned to spend time in her room when no one else was home. I want to scream at him, throw him out, send him away. But I don't. I feel as though he deserves something in return for having given a small chunk of his Isabelle to me, a fragment of a moment that had been lost to me.

Grandma Régine is lurking in a corner. She is listening closely even though she's pretending not to. I call out to her that I'm going to show Ron Johnson Isabelle's room. She gives me a look that says she didn't realize that Isabelle's room has become a museum or a mausoleum, but she doesn't stop me.

I get up and Ron Johnson follows me. I feel his eyes on the back of my neck. His stare feels so intense that it's almost like a slight touch.

I turn around, and he smiles when he sees the STAY OUT sign on Isabelle's door.

"You didn't think she was hostile, did you?" I say as I open the door.

"Actually no," he says.

"That was mostly for our parents," I say.

"Should I take off my shoes?" he asks.

"It's not Mecca," I say as I turn on the light.

He walks in slowly, carefully, squinting behind his glasses as though he were tiptoeing into a dark cave. He methodically takes in the room, perhaps comparing what he's seeing to what he's imagined. He looks up at the seashell chandelier, then down at her bookcase headboard.

"May I?" he asks, once again sounding like an old man.

"Feel free," I say.

He sits on the edge of her bed and reaches over to the bookcase. He flips through a few of Isabelle's old magazines. Some yellowed subscription cards fall out, and he picks them up and puts them back as though they were precious artifacts from another age, which in a way they are.

He walks over to her daybed and runs his fingers over the railing. He picks up the mason jars full of buttons and holds them up, close to his glasses. He turns each of the jars around and examines the buttons as though he knows exactly what they meant to her, to us. Growing in size as we did. Changing in styles and colors with our ages. Getting plainer as we grew older: from cartoon characters' faces to basic black, white, red, and grey.

He is looking at our buttons as though they are lit up, or

are buzzing around inside those jars. He's looking at our buttons like he knows everything about her, about us, like he's family.

When he puts the jars down, his gaze wanders over to the music sheets on the wall. He reaches up and touches one of them, closes his eyes, and effortlessly traces the notes with his fingers, all while humming the wordless melody.

"Florence Beatrice Price, Symphony in E Minor," he says. He looks as though he is reading something in braille.

Florence Beatrice Price was the first black woman to have one of her symphonies performed by a major orchestra in the United States. Isabelle's orchestra teacher, Ms. Backer, promised Isabelle that the school orchestra would perform the Price symphony at next year's spring concert, which would have been—should have been—Isabelle's last one at the school.

Ron keeps humming the most repetitive and somber parts of the symphony. He is, I realize, a music person, too.

As soon as he stops humming, he opens his eyes and slides his finger over to Izzie's wall calendar with the day of this year's concert circled in red. His index finger follows the red circle around and around several times. I know the Price symphony is still playing in his head, because it is playing in mine, too. I've heard Isabelle blast it dozens of times. Some parts of it are muted, but it's mostly upbeat.

Ron then walks over to the picture of him and Isabelle with the whales on the beach. Their smiles take up most of the frame. He does not look at the picture for long.

He covers his face with his hands and sobs.

I keep myself from crying by imagining how sweet Isabelle would have found all of this, how absolutely and positively over-the-top romantic. I could have teased her about it for years, but it would have made her day. It would have made her month. It would have made her life.

He wipes the tears with the back of his hand, looks up, and says, "I'm sorry."

"No problem," I say.

"I think I'm going to go now," he says.

I offer him the picture of him and Isabelle, but he refuses it.

"I have one, too," he says.

He walks out of the room ahead of me, and it is my turn to follow him.

Grandma Régine is waiting for us in the living room.

"Is everything all right?" she asks us both.

"Yes," I say. But I am lying. Nothing will ever be all right again. I walk Ron Johnson to our front door. Another part of my heart splinters off, then shatters as I close the door behind him. I now know that he and my sister shared much more than one blissful day watching stranded whales at the beach.

This is the only important secret she's ever tried to keep from me.

"Will he become a nuisance?" Grandma Régine asks.

Somehow I don't think so. Ron Johnson now knows that I fully understand what he meant to Isabelle. And he has said goodbye to both of us.

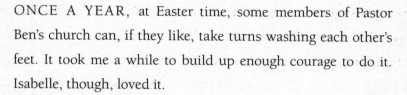

CHAPTER 27

ONCE A YEAR, at Easter time, some members of Pastor Ben's church can, if they like, take turns washing each other's feet. It took me a while to build up enough courage to do it. Isabelle, though, loved it.

First of all, I don't have pretty feet. Isabelle's feet were not that pretty, either, but at least she'd wear socks around the house to both hide and protect them. My thick soles were only part of the reason I'd avoided the Easter foot-washing service. The other reason is that I think it's yucky.

Foot washing, Pastor Ben explains on Easter Sunday morning, is common in many ancient cultures, where it's considered courteous to wash the feet of one's visitors. Usually the visitor has traveled long and dusty distances in sandals and is in need of a good scrub. I remind myself of this as my parents and Aunt

Leslie and Grandpa Marcus and Grandma Régine keep bugging me to enter one of the smaller rooms, a plain white one, where the foot washing is to take place. When I walk in, Tina is sitting on a stool behind a white plastic washbasin.

"Did you pick me on purpose?" I ask.

"My grandpa's the minister. I get first dibs on all the best feet." Her laughter echoes through the room.

Tina is an old pro at foot washing. She motions for me to sit on the chair facing her. I push off my flat, roomy shoes and let my feet sway above the water.

"Are you mad at me or something?" she asks.

"Are we supposed to talk while doing this?" I ask.

We are not supposed to talk. We are actually supposed to be praying, asking God to reveal to us our most humble selves, our deepest sense of service to others.

Tina guides my feet into the basin, cups the warm water by the handfuls, and pours it over my toes. Pulling my feet deeper into the basin, she gently massages my arches.

"Jean Michel says you're not calling him, either," she says.

"Does he, now?"

"My mom says when you hit your head as hard as you did, you get a lot of mood swings, so I'm going to forgive you now."

"Bite me," I say.

"I would if your feet weren't so gross," she says.

"I miss Isabelle, too," she adds, after pouring a few more handfuls of water on my toes. "I loved her, too."

Once, when Tina was hanging out with us at the house, she was doing what she calls "twin testing" and asked Isabelle and me to write down what our last meal would be, if we were on death row. Our imagined maximum security prison was on a strict budget, so we could only pick three things.

Isabelle asked Tina to jot down the menu for her last supper and it turns out that the three of us mostly had the same things: a really big burger, some curly sweet potato fries, and each of us a different kind of milk shake. I'd tried not to choose something Isabelle would go for, so I'd opted for Tina's favorite meal. Isabelle must have mind-read my choice. Isabelle's one extra thing was Grandma Régine's vanilla coconut cake, which she said she'd ask Tina and me to sneak past the guards for her.

"Double bite me," I tell Tina for making me remember this, too.

We switch places and now it's my turn at her feet, which, unlike mine, are well manicured. I give her feet a real scrubbing, but do not put them between my teeth and bite them, pinch her, draw blood, or bring her to tears, which is what I want to do.

Foot washing is supposed to be a shared experience of surrender, as Pastor Ben liked to say. I just hadn't expected it to be a make-up session with my friend.

"It might have been easier to do this for a leper," Tina says once we're done.

We hug.

"Are we okay now?" she asks.

"We're okay now," I say.

"When are you coming back to school?" she asks.

"I don't know," I say. Both my parents agree with Aunt Leslie that I'm not yet ready to go back.

Tina and I sit together on a side pew and watch as Dad and Mom try to wash each other's feet. Mom's bandages have been getting smaller and smaller, and underneath her elaborate hats her hair is starting to grow again. Her ribs are hurting less, too. She's not grimacing as much when she moves, and she's able to bend down and get up for the foot washing.

Dad now has his wounded arm in a sling, but is still wearing his leg cast, so Mom only washes one of his feet. When it's Dad's turn, Mom has to sit on a higher stool and one of the deacons has to hold the basin, which shows you how much effort they're both putting into this. Dad strokes Mom's feet in the water and tickles her toes with his good hand and they smile to each other as he does it.

If only Isabelle could see this, I think.

"I'm astonished," she'd say.

CHAPTER 28

ASIDE FROM THE crash articles online, Gloria Carlton is nowhere to be found. Before she leaves town to go pack her things, Aunt Leslie finds thirty or so Carltons in the Miami-Dade area. She calls them all. None of the Carltons she gets to speak to her—by blocking her phone number and pretending to be a high school principal—have a daughter named Gloria.

Since Ron Johnson dropped by unannounced, Mom agrees to let Tina and Jean Michel come over one day after school.

Jean Michel and Tina spend the afternoon on their laptops, combing the Internet for clues to Gloria Carlton's past. Though I still get light-sensitivity headaches, I'm now able to look at screens with my cat eyes without feeling like my eyeballs are being stabbed with needles. Still, Jean Michel keeps reminding me to be careful, as though I've just left the hospital.

Jean Michel and I don't act the same way around each other anymore. He's less flirtatious with me now, a lot more cautious. Maybe he's responding to the ways I have changed, the way I can't even imagine being playful, or even being fully myself, with him or anybody else.

Things haven't been the same with Tina, either. How can they be? With Isabelle gone, I have no right to do the same things Tina does, to go on with my life just like it was before. But I need their help and I'm glad they agreed to help me.

I get tired really fast, so we don't get too far with the search. They promise to work on it at home and come back with some answers for me the next day.

"These Carltons," Tina says, mimicking a James Bond–type British accent, "are definitely trying not to be found."

When they come back the next afternoon, Jean Michel gets on his laptop to plug in some new tools that he and Tina have researched.

I notice as he logs on that his screen saver is Frida Kahlo's *The Two Fridas*.

How does he know, I wonder, that this is exactly how I've been feeling? Split in half sometimes, and at other times walking, living, breathing for two. Two hearts are beating in my one chest, but it feels like no heart at all.

Mr. Rhys would call this a moment of sentimental appropriation. Just like the grief class he tried to have for me.

"I think we got it," Jean Michel says, typing the Fridas away. "It took us most of the night—"

"Working remotely," Tina clarifies.

"And our lunch periods today." Jean Michel completes his thought.

"I can't wait for you to see this." Tina lets out a joyful shriek.

This is her big reveal.

Their excitement for me, more than being pleased with themselves, tells me that they really want me to have some answers, to be a little bit at peace.

Tina lets Jean Michel do all the typing, but it seems like they're onto something together. Using their newly acquired software and apps, they found out something non-crash-related about a girl from Miami named Gloria Carlton.

Jean Michel then shows me a portrait of Gloria Carlton on our school photographer's website. He morphs that picture with a screenshot of the picture Officer Sanchez showed me, the one from the newspaper. Tina imports that blended picture into a bunch of school databases. Hundreds of wrong faces pop up quickly until the screen slows down, then freezes, and we get our highest read, 85 percent recognition, on a matching image for our girl.

The new picture is maybe a year old. Gloria Carlton is standing at the entrance of a school near downtown Miami called Midtown Academy. She's wearing a school uniform, khaki pants, and a white blouse. Underneath that picture is the name Janice Hill.

"I swear we could work for the FBI," Tina tells Jean Michel.

No wonder this took them most of the night, and their lunch hour, too.

It's all moving faster than my bruised brain and racing heart can keep up with, though. Is it possible that they found something about Gloria Carlton that the police hadn't?

"We should give this information to the police," I say.

"They can't figure out that we hacked into the Board of Ed records," Tina says.

I have never seen this side of Tina before. It's a cooler, bolder, more dangerous version of Tina.

"I found her birth records," she tells me.

She's sweating now, every pore on her face bursting wet.

The links to the birth records show that Janice Hill was born in Gainesville, Florida. She's actually sixteen and not fourteen.

"Maybe she and her family are in the witness protection program," Tina says, "and now she's just blown it. She'll have to get a different identity."

Jean Michel chortles. Their eyes linger on each other's. I feel like a third wheel.

I ask Tina to send what they've found out to my mom's and dad's email addresses. My head is throbbing again from all the screen gazing, so I ask them to leave so I can lie down, close my eyes, and process all this for a while.

Still, I can't stop thinking about their discovery. How come Officer Butler and Officer Sanchez hadn't figured out that Gloria Carlton was an alias?

CHAPTER 29

GRANDMA RÉGINE AND Grandpa Marcus are out for their early evening walk. My parents are fighting.

They shut the bedroom door, but I can still hear everything they're saying. I guess foot washing can't save every relationship.

One of them must have opened the door, then slammed it shut, then opened it again. Mom is screaming so loud that I'm worried someone might hear her from the street and call the police.

I stumble out of my room and into the hallway. Both Mom and Dad are standing there, looking breathless, with their backs pressed against the wall.

Dad is leaning on his crutches while holding a letter and envelope. He looks up and sees me standing there, then goes back to mouthing the words from the letter to himself. Then he hands the letter to me.

"She's not supposed to be reading." Mom grabs the letter back from me.

"She just sent us an email," Dad says.

"That was my friend," I say.

"We sent it to the officers," Mom says.

"What's this letter?" I ask.

"It's a thank-you letter for organ donations," Dad says.

"And they're thanking us for your corneas and your heart."

My corneas? *My* heart?

"We'd already signed the papers when we thought it was you," Dad says.

Every word coming out of both their mouths is spat out with anger. Their anger is not really directed at each other, though, but at the entire situation, at yet another reminder that Isabelle is gone. But it sure seems like they hate each other.

I need to back up. They donated Isabelle's heart and eyes and did not even mention it to me. So I'm wrong about the time Isabelle died. Maybe she actually died, really died, when her organs were put into those other people.

Still, I can't help but like the idea that parts of Isabelle are still out there somewhere. She did not just smolder into ashes. Her heart is beating in someone else's chest. Her corneas are looking at things. They're seeing flowers, clouds, stars.

"Izzie's heart is inside somebody else," Mom says, rocking herself.

Dad tries to reach over and put his arms around her, but she pulls away, almost letting him fall. He balances himself quickly, grabbing the crutches and pushing back against the wall.

"Izzie's heart is inside somebody else," Mom keeps saying.

"You signed the papers," Dad says. "We both signed all the papers. You said Iz would have wanted it that way."

"I know," Mom said. "*M konnen.*"

Isabelle's heart is in somebody else's body.

It's starting to sink in now.

Isabelle's eyes and heart are in other people.

"Are we going to know who the people are?" I ask.

"We said we were open to hearing from them," Dad says.

Them. My now partial twins? Mom and Dad's now partial children? No matter how old they are. Or maybe it doesn't even work that way.

I wonder where these people live, what languages they speak. Would having Isabelle's heart mean that this person would love us, too? Would her corneas make the person who receives them want to see us, to be sure we're okay?

"Remember you said it yourself that night," Dad reminds Mom. "What if one of the girls needed a heart?"

"I know what I said," Mom snaps back. "Doesn't make it easier now."

They don't usually have full-blown fights in front of me, but now they seem to forget that I'm even standing there.

"Just don't make it sound like I decided this on my own," Dad says.

"I'm not angry," Mom yells. "*M pa fache.*"

Even though it sounds like she is.

"I know what I agreed to," she says. "But now I've changed my mind. I want it back. I want her heart back. I want her eyes back. I want all of her back."

"Do you realize how crazy that sounds?" Dad asks. "*Ou fou?*"

"No crazier than her being dead," Mom says. "Yes, I want all of her back."

"Please," Dad says. "Can we just sit and talk about this in a reasonable way?"

"There's nothing reasonable about this situation," Mom says.

"They told us to expect to feel conflicted," Dad says.

"Conflicted? Are you kidding me? Conflicted?"

Mom walks back into their bedroom and slams the door shut behind her.

All the shouting and the door-slamming makes me feel like a giant mirror has just been smashed over my head.

"Are you all right?" Dad asks.

"I should lie down," I say.

"Sorry you had to see that," he says.

Even though Mom's upset, I know Isabelle would have been

thrilled about living on in somebody else's body, if that's what you can even call it.

"Iz would have approved," I say. "She would have loved what you guys have done."

"That was our feeling," he says.

Isabelle's body is now a nebula. It's expanded into other spheres, other spaces. Her heart and corneas have been wept over, hoped and prayed for, even while they were still in her body. And even though she'd been broken that night, shattered, parts of her had landed somewhere safe.

CHAPTER 30

THE NEXT MORNING, Officer Butler and Officer Sanchez drop by. Gloria Carlton/Janice Hill and her parents have disappeared.

After they received that email and a phone call from Dad, the officers went over to their apartment to ask them some questions and found out that they'd packed up and left.

The police still had their minivan, and found no other cars registered in their names either as Carltons or Hills. There were warrants put out for their arrests, but for now the police had no idea where they were.

We all huddle around the officers—Mom and Dad, Grandma Régine and Grandpa Marcus, and me—getting the details.

"Something strange is going on," Officer Butler says. "Your

tip was legit. The girl has several aliases and so do the parents. If they are her parents."

I couldn't wait to tell Jean Michel and Tina that they had Nancy Drewed it and cracked the case.

Grandpa Marcus mutters something in Creole. He pats his jacket where he keeps his cigarettes. Of everything he says, the only thing I understand is something he repeats over and over.

"*Twòp. Twòp.* Too much. This is too much."

Grandma Régine points to the sliding glass door leading to the back porch, quietly suggesting that Grandpa Marcus step out before he gets more upset.

"What's next?" Dad asks once Grandpa Marcus is gone.

"We're going to find them," Officer Butler says. "Both for your family's sake and the sake of that girl. She might be in danger."

"You think they might be holding the girl against her will?" Dad asks.

"We have to get her back here so she can answer some questions," Officer Sanchez says.

Grandpa Marcus is still muttering under his breath when he returns from smoking his cigarette. He looks even more agitated than before. Grandma Régine follows him to the kitchen and takes out a kettle to make him some tea.

"We wanted to come and tell you what's happening before it hits the news," Officer Butler says. Her voice hasn't changed much since I heard it for the first time in the hospital. It's still an emotionless monotone.

Grandpa Marcus walks the officers to the door.

"Find those crazies," he says.

I rush to the kitchen phone to call Tina. I forgot that it's Sunday. Tina's in church, but she answers anyway.

When I ask her if she can step out and patch in Jean Michel, she says, "We came out to answer the phone."

"We?"

"Me and Jean Michel."

"Really?"

"He's right here next to me," she says. "This morning he called and said he wanted to visit our church."

I hang up. But why? They hadn't told me that they were planning to go to church together.

I don't answer the phone when they call back. I have bigger things to think about. When they call me again, I tell Grandma Régine to tell them I'm napping.

My parents' fight continues.

"We should offer a reward," Mom shouts, "so they can find these people."

"Let the police do their jobs," Dad says.

"And what do we do?" Mom asks.

"You want me to hire a professional killer?" Dad asks, escalating his sarcasm game. "Or do you want me to go find them and kill them myself?"

"You can get Moy to put more pressure on the police," Mom says.

Grandpa Marcus steps between them, and they limp and hobble to different corners of the house.

When Dessalines curls himself around my feet, I grab him, put on my cat eyes, and walk out to the backyard with him in my arms. Sitting in the shade, on the pool deck, I can't help but feel like he is my only friend. That is, until he dashes off yet again.

Our backyard is practically a pet cemetery. Buried there are Dessalines's predecessors: a turtle named Pétion—we called him Pete—a rabbit named Toussaint, a guinea pig named Jefferson, an iguana named Lincoln, and a few random squirrels we'd found dead in the yard.

Dessalines ignores me still, so I walk into the garage alone. My parents don't use the garage for cars unless we're going away for a while. They mostly park on the street, in front of the house.

The walls of the garage are covered from floor to ceiling with boxes filled with our old things, ancient clothes and other mementos that Mom and Dad can't part with. There are some new boxes full of cards and stuffed animals, and even some prayer rugs and healing quilts that Mrs. Clifton and her quilting group had made for us.

Against the back wall are four stacks of Grandma Sandrine's paintings. I remember seeing them in her apartment when she was living there and later in the chapel at her wake. They look a lot different now, the ones I can see, the paint having settled into the canvases, which are wrapped up in plastic.

I can only see the four up front, but they're pretty typical of Grandma Sandrine's style. One looks like a bowl of spaghetti. The other looks like a bunch of random coffee stains. The third seems a bit more planned. There is a red circle in the middle of the large canvas and a bunch of bloody-looking feet (Grandma Sandrine's feet?) walking away from that circle.

The last one is my favorite. Grandma Sandrine cut out and pasted hundreds of faces of brown-skinned old women from newspapers and magazines and collaged them into one massive head, which she then split right down the middle with a line of thick black paint. This was one of her last paintings before she couldn't paint anymore. Isabelle and I have always thought that it showed how torn she felt between wanting to live and wanting to die.

CHAPTER 31

GRANDMA RÉGINE AND Grandpa Marcus take me to my scheduled appointment with Dr. Rosemay the next day. I am so over doctors—even Dr. Rosemay—that I willingly apply my short-term memory loss option to those visits.

Dr. Rosemay asks if I'm depressed.

I don't know what she's expecting me to say, but I say no so I can get out of there faster.

It used to be so nice to come see her when the worst thing that had ever happened to me was having a bad ear infection.

She gives me an eye test, a hearing test, and goes over all the cognitive things again, the counting backwards, the walking backwards. Now I just want to block her out, too.

That is until she says something I've been waiting to hear for a while.

After examining me, Dr. Rosemay says I should probably rule out going back to school for the rest of the school year. Not because I'm getting worse. I'm actually getting better, but summer is only a few short weeks away and the effort of trying to catch up would be too much. She's going to call Dr. Aidoo and Mom and Dad and recommend that I go to summer school instead.

I don't see how my parents could deny me that, given all that's happened. Besides, my mind isn't going to be on English and math, French and social studies, or even art, anyway. It's going to be on Isabelle, and on my parents' fights, on Janice Hill's disappearance, and on Tina and Jean Michel growing closer to each other and further away from me.

When we get home from the doctor's office, we find Mom and Dad sitting at the kitchen table with Isabelle's urn between them. The urn reminds me of a copper teapot, without the spout.

Isabelle's full name, Isabelle Régine Boyer, is carved into it along with the dates of her birth and death, which is one of the days I was under.

When we join them at the table, Grandma Régine's eyes fill up with tears. She's the one who picked out this urn.

When you're a twin, people tend to think that you're most like only one other person on earth. Isabelle had a bit of all of us in her, but a whole lot of Grandma Régine. Both she and

Grandma Régine wanted to carve their own paths, but were never fully sure how to clearly express it.

We all sit there for what seems like hours, and we stare at the urn until the kitchen phone rings.

Grandpa Marcus walks over and picks it up. He holds the phone away from his mouth and says to Mom, "It's your friend. Madame Marshall."

"Tell her I'll call her later," Mom says.

"*Elle dit que c'est urgent*," Grandpa Marcus says. "She says to turn on the news."

Mom takes the urn with her as she walks over to the living room. Dad follows, hobbling behind us on his crutches. Grandpa Marcus turns on the TV.

I know it's serious because no one is telling me not to look at the TV. Grandpa Marcus flips through the channels until he lands in the middle of the four o'clock news.

Even before hearing the newscaster's voice, we see the scroll.

BREAKING NEWS: TEEN TWIN KILLER CAUGHT

They make it sound like there's been a manhunt when actually Janice Hill and her parents were simply identified by a Greyhound bus driver on a bus heading to Atlanta. The bus driver called the police, and the police pulled the bus over and arrested them. This, I realize, is probably how most mysteries are solved, by ordinary people, rather than the Nancy Drew way. The police cruiser was trailed by a news van, so the entire thing was recorded for TV.

In the footage of the family getting off the bus, Janice doesn't look nervous at all. She even smiles a little, a restrained but real smile. A smile of relief.

Maybe I'm the only who sees it, but she looks like someone who's taking a deep breath. And when one of the reporters shoves a microphone in her face and asks, "What do you have to say to Isabelle Boyer's family?" She looks up for a moment and stares directly into the camera. Her eyes get all cloudy and her lips tremble. She takes another deep breath, then says in a very soft voice, "I would change places with her if I could."

Except for the sound of her voice, there is total silence around me. Her voice is so soft that the reporter has to repeat her words.

Later, when that clip is played over and over again, the news stations will add subtitles so everyone can understand what she says.

I imagine being one of those reporters and having a chance to ask her another question.

"What exactly do you mean when you say that you would trade places with Isabelle?" I'd ask.

"I would die instead," I'd make her say. "I would crash into a wall somewhere, not into Isabelle, and it would be my head that would smash into the glass, not Isabelle's, and my organs, and not hers, would be in other people's bodies right now."

I'd make her say all this, because that's what I want to say about myself, too.

I don't know why, but I believe her. I believe she means what she says to that reporter, that she would change places with Isabelle if she could. I need to believe something, anything. So I believe her.

After all, aren't we equally guilty, Janice and me?

If we'd left the house fifteen minutes earlier, we would have missed her altogether.

When the news broadcast moves on to another even more gruesome subject, Mom groans loudly.

Dad lowers his head. Grandpa Marcus and Grandma Régine reach for each other's hands.

Before the newscast is even over, people start calling us non-stop. Aunt Leslie calls from Orlando. Uncle Patrick from New York. Alejandra from Los Angeles. Mrs. Marshall and Tina show up at our door, along with a couple of news trucks and half the neighborhood.

"You didn't have to come," Dad says to all of them.

Then, looking at the urn in my mother's arms, Mrs. Marshall and a few people say, "Oh, yes we did. We certainly had to come."

Tina and I haven't spoken to each other since that Sunday she and Jean Michel went to church together. I have less and less to say to everyone now, including her. I don't have much strength or energy left for it.

As the house fills up with people, I close my eyes, allowing our visitors to float around me. Every now and then, though, I open my eyes and see more people there. Some of the people are stroking the urn in Mom's arms as Dad unsuccessfully tries to pry it away from her.

The light outside grows dimmer as the house becomes more crowded, and I'm not even sure anymore whether it's dawn or dusk, whether I'm myself or Isabelle, whether I'm at home or still in that car again, heading to the spring orchestra concert on a Friday afternoon just like this one.

Soon the light coming through the windows fades. Grandpa Marcus and Grandma Régine turn on the house lights, and I realize that this moment of suddenly going from semi-darkness to nearly blinding light unexpectedly feels a lot like the crash.

At this very hour that Friday evening, Isabelle was supposed to arrive at the school auditorium, say hi to her friends, warm up with her flute, then go onstage and play one of her favorite pieces of music with the school orchestra.

In one corner of the room, I see Moy talking to Dad. Maybe Commissioner Moy, as we now call him, had something to do with the police working so hard on our case. Maybe he did and maybe he didn't, but Dad sure seems happy to see him. They are smiling and shaking hands, almost doing victory fist pumps.

On the other side of the room, I see Tina and Jean Michel standing together and talking, and I'm not even angry at them. I'm not mad. I'm not even jealous of the little sparks going off between them, sparks they may not even realize are there.

Tina and Jean Michel are doing something I can't even think of doing right now. Their lives are taking them somewhere I'm not able to go. Besides, maybe if I hadn't been so concerned about looking pretty for Jean Michel that night, my sister might still be alive. Tina and Jean Michel and all these people crowding around me now all feel like something out of a nightmare, something I need to leave behind. They all feel pentimento.

One of the possible lifelong effects of hitting my head so hard in the car, Dr. Aidoo told Aunt Leslie and me during our most recent visit with him, is that I might develop something called pseudobulbar affect, a neurological condition that might make me laugh, or cry, or both, suddenly, out of the blue.

Sitting there in the living room, with all of those people around me, I feel something like that coming. A *fou rire*, or crazy laugh, as my grandparents would call it, the kind of mixed laughing and crying Isabelle and I sometimes saw people do at funerals, in the cathedrals that Grandpa Marcus would take us to in Haiti. The grief was always intense, but sometimes you couldn't tell whether people were laughing or crying. It was as if both their joy and their sadness were coming from the same spot, as if losing someone had temporarily fused every nerve in their brains together.

I try my best to force my laughter and tears to cancel each other out. So all I'm left with is a kind of numbness, an Amazon-length river running through that empty cave inside of me.

I keep wondering what Isabelle would be doing now if she were sitting here in my place. Maybe she'd be vowing to go out and fight a war for me. Maybe she'd be losing it and yelling at everyone, asking them to leave. Her *fou rire* would have probably crushed this numbness I can't shake.

We keep the TV on and watch the news repeat itself. Each time a news anchor or reporter mentions Isabelle, he or she says that Isabelle is "survived" by us, her family.

She is survived by her mother, father, and her twin sister.

"Survived by" doesn't sound quite right.

How can she be survived by us?

By some strange twist of fate that killed her, we came out all right. *We* survived. She had removed her seat belt for a minute and her head had smashed into the car window, but we had survived.

Finally, Tina and Jean Michel come over and sit next to me. Maybe I would feel better if Tina, Jean Michel, and I had solved the entire mystery together. Maybe I would be happier if we had figured out every single part of it, all the way through.

The other piece of breaking news is that, just as Officer Butler and Officer Sanchez had suspected, the people who'd been arrested with Janice were not her parents. Her most recent foster family had run off with her, then had given her to these other people, after putting an ad on a website. Janice had taken this new couple's minivan and was trying to escape from them that Friday night.

I keep waiting for this to make total sense to me. I keep hoping for it to offer some relief, some serenity, some deep sense of satisfaction. I want to be celebrating something. Bad people have been caught. A lost girl has been rescued and saved. A grey wolf? A princess? A firebird? But Isabelle has not been rescued. Isabelle is still gone. She's still in the urn that Mom keeps glued to her body.

Maybe we've had too much and others too little. Who says we deserve joy when others constantly live in pain? Who says we must have a good life when others are riding with death every single day?

My heart is so crushed that I don't even know how to be glad for Janice. My sister's gone and my friends seem to be falling in love. Janice has survived, but I'm being left behind.

I have no desire to explain what I'm feeling. I have no one to explain it to who would fully understand. Only Isabelle would have understood.

Isabelle would have also understood that no one has won here. These types of celebrations are temporary anyway. Judging by Mom's disappearing into her office with that urn, the survivors are too busy trying to figure out what to do with their dead.

CHAPTER 32

I START DRAWING again after Dr. Aidoo tells me I can. Usually I like to draw people alone in a wide landscape, something I find quick and easy to do.

One of my favorite things to draw is a person walking alone on a beach in the middle of the day, when the sun is at its highest point in the sky. I usually spend more time drawing the shadow than the person, because shadows are a lot more interesting to me. I like the way you can stretch or shrink them based on the light source.

My ninth-grade art teacher, Ms. Walker, used to say that to be good at drawing you need to simplify. You have to break things down into small parts, into lines, dashes, and dots. Bodies become shapes. Faces become circles. Chests become squares. Legs become cylinders and cones.

My favorite part of drawing has always been shading, filling in a pencil outline by adding darker and darker layers for more depth. I also love drawing broken things.

"Ruins," Ms. Walker said, "are a lot easier to draw than perfect things."

And here I am surrounded by ruins.

I begin by sketching our backyard, starting with the mango and avocado trees, then adding the new red hibiscus bushes, jasmines, and crocuses that Grandma Régine had planted. Then I draw the kidney-shaped pool and the deck where Grandma Régine and Grandpa Marcus are lounging next to each other, their faces covered with wide-brimmed straw-colored sun hats.

Grandpa Marcus is wearing green swim shorts and Grandma Régine a matching monokini. They're quietly taking in the sun, while also watching my parents, who are sitting across from them, on the other side of the pool, fully dressed, in the shade.

Mom's head is almost completely healed, the scar on her forehead getting less and less visible every day. Dad is still going around on his crutches but is wearing a lighter sling on his arm and a medical boot on his leg. He will be starting physical therapy soon.

Before, when I would try to sketch a moment like this—a still and uncomfortable moment—if Isabelle was there, she'd turn around and look at me now and then, waving as if to a camera to make sure I could see her. So I sketch Isabelle in. I sketch her right in the middle of my ruins.

Later I will shade her in. I'll draw her doing a breaststroke in the pool, and I will draw myself sitting on the edge of the pool watching her. I will fill all of us in, watching Isabelle swimming. I'll even add Dessalines lurking in a corner somewhere.

While trying to frame and sketch all of this, I keep wishing there was some way to make it come even more alive and feel more real. So I drop the sketch pad, and when no one is looking, I slip into the pool. And while doing my breaststroke, I don't feel dizzy. I don't sink under. I don't drown.

Mom and Dad and Grandpa Marcus and Grandma Régine get up and move to the edge of the pool. At first they look frightened. Then on their faces I see something that looks a little bit like wonder. Like, wow. She is doing this. She is really here. Even though her sister is not.

One day I'll be able to sketch myself alone. One day, I will be able to draw myself as no longer a twin, as the *dosa*, the untwinned one. The untwined one. But not just yet.

CHAPTER 33

BETWEEN MOM AND Dad, Dad is the first to go back to work. He's still not able to drive, so a partner from his law firm picks him up in the morning, then brings him home in the late afternoon. Someone from his office also takes him to his doctor's appointments and physical therapy sessions.

In spite of what Aunt Leslie said, his life is already moving on, outside of the house, away from us.

Dad has always seemed calmer when he's working. Mom, who one might think has the more fun job, always looks tense when she's leaving for work.

Being around so many news people must have finally gotten to her, so one day while we're eating a lavish dinner of rice and beans and stewed conch that Grandma Régine has cooked for us, Mom announces that she quit her job. And this time for good.

She's not sure what she's going to do next, but she doesn't want to do makeup anymore.

"I think I might go back to school," she says.

She's not sure what she wants to study.

She sounds like one of my friends, one who doesn't know which Advanced Placement classes to take.

"I have a sister who's a doctor," she says. "It can't be that hard."

"No one ever said you couldn't do anything you wanted to do," Dad says.

Then Mom just tunes out everyone else and starts speaking to me.

"What would you do if you were me, Gizzie?"

She tosses the question off lightly, but I take it seriously.

I want to tell her to not change a thing, to keep her same job, and to stay married to Dad. So much has changed, I want to say, why don't we just keep everything else the same?

I can't bring myself to say that, though, because I don't want the same things, either. I want to move away for one thing, far away from everything that's happened.

"Marriages change," Mom declares to all of us. "And as we learned recently, life is short. So I'm not going miss any of it."

Grandma Régine and Grandpa Marcus put their forks down at the same time and stare at Mom. Both their mouths are open, aghast. They look totally flabbergasted, like the mystified parents of an insolent child.

Some people never get to grow up. Others never stop growing up. My mother, I realize, is still trying to grow up. Whatever other dreams she'd had, she'd given up to take care of Isabelle and me, and she did her best to protect us from feeling guilty by never even mentioning what those dreams were. I never fully understood or appreciated that side of her until I had to watch her try to defend it.

"I didn't realize you've been missing out on your life," Dad says. He sounds all choked up, like he's fighting back tears.

"I need to live a little bit more for myself," Mom says. "Just like I told you before all this happened."

So the separation was her idea.

Hearing all this makes me think back to a few months earlier when Mom and Dad and Isabelle and I were at the Pérez Art Museum Miami, looking at some Chinese vases on a raised platform on the floor. Some of the vases were over two thousand years old. They had been painted in bright and pastel colors by the Chinese artist Ai Weiwei and the pamphlets we were carrying around said that they were valued at a million dollars each.

We'd spent nearly an hour looking at all sixteen of the vases, with Dad saying that the paint had defaced them, reducing their value as artifacts. Mom liked that they were painted over and saw it as a sign of renewal. Isabelle was barely hanging in there, doing her best not to bolt for the nearest exit to go meet her friends at the mall.

Just as we were heading out of the room, a man walked in, picked up one of the vases, and dropped it on the floor, smashing it to pieces. The man then stood quietly and waited for the police to come and arrest him.

As two policemen handcuffed him, he told them that he was an artist himself and that he had been staging a protest against the museum. Others saw what he had done as live art. A couple of tourists even clapped.

This was the last time we'd all had an outing together before that evening in the car.

It's hard to not keep thinking of lasts.

Isabelle used to say that for good things, you think of firsts. For bad things, you think of lasts.

These are the first things I want to remember, the last things I want to forget:

Sometimes Isabelle would read a book backwards. She would start with the last chapter and work her way to the front so that she could first read about the characters after their lives had changed. Isabelle loved road trips. She wanted to learn to ski. She hated hot dogs and the sound of blow-dryers, and she was always the first one to jump in the pool at anybody's pool party. Holding your breath to play the flute was a lot like holding your breath to swim or dive, she always said.

The last time I saw Tina and Jean Michel together, I asked them both to meet me at the Pérez museum where Ai Weiwei's fifteen remaining vases were still on display, with some new heavy-duty motion detectors and a few more security guards.

Grandpa Marcus and Grandma Régine drove me there, but they went to check out a Caribbean art exhibit while I spoke to my friends amidst the invisible ruins of Ai Weiwei's broken vase.

I wasn't sure that they needed it, but I gave Tina and Jean Michel my blessing.

"I'm going to tell you both this just once, then we'll never have to mention it again," I said, as they stood on either side of me, shifting their weight from one leg to the other, fidgeting.

The words didn't exactly come freely, but I tried to tell them that whatever was going on with them, they wouldn't be smashing my heart, like that artist had smashed Ai Weiwei's million-dollar vase. My heart was already in a million pieces. No one, or nothing, could ever shatter it again, the way losing Isabelle had.

They both looked as distraught as I felt, and neither one seemed to know what to say next.

"I don't ever want to love anyone again the way I love Isabelle" is really what I wanted to say. Instead I told them that as soon as I'm cleared for travel, I will go spend the summer with my grandparents in Haiti. Then in September, even if it means graduating later than Isabelle and I were supposed to— especially if it means graduating later than Isabelle and I were supposed to—I'm moving to New York to intern at Uncle Patrick's new label and live with him and Alejandra while I finish high school in Brooklyn.

They both held their hands out to me, as if to keep me from falling. But I wasn't falling. I was deep inside my chrysalis and I was waiting to be transformed into some kind of hypoallergenic butterfly.

"You're wrong," I heard them say.

"We're not!" they shouted at the same time.

Their simultaneous denial startled them, too. Jean Michel's mouth stayed open, as though thousands of jumbled-up words were invisibly pouring out. Tina's face crumpled up like paper, even as she was fighting to keep it intact. She was doing her best not to cry, and so was I.

Then after the most pregnant of all pregnant pauses, Tina muttered something under her breath and all I heard was "Whatever." Then Jean Michel echoed her with "Yeah, whatever." And maybe just so he could keep talking to me, he proceeded to tell me in a suddenly cool and unflustered-sounding voice that helping to find Janice made him think that he's a better computer geek than a visual artist, so rather than a summer art program, he was going to take a bunch of computer classes at the University of Miami.

Tina, following his cue, said in her best church-announcement voice that she was going to stay in town, too, to work summer camp with Pastor Ben at the church.

Sometimes you just have to know when to let go. Still, as both Tina and Jean Michel were talking, I kept thinking to myself, "Wait until Isabelle hears about this stupid decision I've just made!" Then I remembered once again that Isabelle was gone.

The last time I heard about Janice Hill was from Officer Butler. Officer Butler came by the house alone one night, in jeans and a T-shirt, to return our phones, Isabelle's backpack, laptop, and flute.

Dad pressed Isabelle's computer against his chest when she handed it to him. I reached for the flute case, and Mom took the rest.

Except for a few scratches on the outside leather, the flute case looked fine. There were no bloodstains on it. Maybe Officer Butler had cleaned it up so that seeing it wouldn't traumatize us so much.

I walked over to the couch and slid the locks open. I ran my fingers over the dark red velvet lining but avoided touching the flute until I remembered that singer Emeline's earring was in one of the dividers underneath the flute.

I wanted to put the flute together and raise it to my lips, just to see what it would sound like. I wanted to ask my parents to time me while I held a note for as long as I could. Just as I'd timed Isabelle hundreds of times. But as many times as I'd watched her do it, I wasn't sure how to assemble the flute, without possibly damaging it.

Instead I raised the flute's body and found Emeline's earring tucked safely in the case's lining. I held the earring in my hand and stroked the tiny metal butterflies, then I put it back in its place.

Neither Mom nor Dad opened the things they were holding, not the laptop or the backpack. Dad looked like he didn't want to ask, but he did.

"What's happening with—"

He couldn't bring himself to say her name.

"Janice?" Officer Butler said.

"Yes," Mom answered.

"She's in a good foster home," Officer Butler said. She was looking more pained than we were, as though she wanted to offer us so much more than that, but couldn't.

"How do you know these people are good?" Mom asked, raising her voice. "How do you know they're not going to traffic that girl again, sell her off to someone else?"

I was thinking the same thing.

"They're not," Officer Butler said. "Even if I have to see to it myself."

I couldn't believe she was reassuring us. About Janice Hill! Or maybe we were all reassuring ourselves.

"Will there be charges?" Dad asked.

"Not against Janice," Officer Butler said.

The state attorney was going to press child trafficking charges against the couples who'd traded Janice online. But due to Janice's extenuating circumstances, Isabelle's death was ruled a very unfortunate accident. Janice wouldn't be getting a driver's license anytime soon, but she wasn't going to jail, either.

The first and last time we heard from Izzie's heart recipient, we received a one-page letter written by hand, in tiny cursive letters.

The night the letter came, I slept in Isabelle's bed with the paper pressed against my chest, just as Mom had held the urn against hers. Somehow, hugging that piece of paper felt more like having Isabelle with me than possibly hearing her phone messages or reading the files on her laptop. I was afraid to read the files on her laptop or listen to her phone messages only to find out that she'd written or said something really mean about me. I didn't want to learn that she secretly hated me, that she sometimes wished I'd never been born.

"I know this is very soon to contact you," a woman, identifying herself only as Roberta ("People call me Bobbie") wrote. "But I can't thank you enough for what you've done for me. I'm twenty-nine years old and I have not had a happy, carefree day in my life since I was twelve. I have never even been in love. My heart has never allowed me to think that I could be. That is until now. Thanks to your daughter Giselle, I was born anew."

Roberta had not gotten the memo that it was Isabelle and not me who'd given her a heart.

One of the many files I eventually find on Isabelle's laptop is a short poem she called "Ron."

I felt you reaching out to me
That night for the first time
To stroke me where time led you.
I loved reaching back to you
Uncoiling myself to fill both your hand
And your heart.

CHAPTER 34

THE FIRST TIME Grandma Régine, Grandpa Marcus, Mom, Dad, Uncle Patrick, Alejandra, Aunt Leslie, Dr. Aidoo, and I are all together again after Isabelle's death is for Isabelle's and my birthday. My family decides to celebrate it, as planned, at Grandpa Marcus and Grandma Régine's house in Haiti.

Once we walk past the passion vines near their front gate, we stop at one of the many spots in the middle of my grandparents' garden, which overlooks the city below.

Grandpa Marcus once showed me and Isabelle the original drawings for the house. He had designed everything around this panoramic view of the mountains, the arbor, and the sea. The wall-to-wall houses on the hillsides and the broken city below had come later, the very rich and the very poor stacking their homes like dominoes, one on top of the other.

Isabelle had loved this garden and this view, because from this spot, she could pretend to hold an entire city, even if a half-broken one, in the palm of her hands. And because Isabelle loved this garden so much, my parents decided to scatter some of her ashes here.

The rest of the ashes would remain at our house in Miami, and later they would travel with us throughout our lives, to places where Isabelle had dreamed of going one day, mostly because she was interested in their music scenes: New Orleans, Dakar, Cape Town, Kingston, Vienna, Saint Petersburg, Bahia, Rio.

We are all standing in the shadow of my grandparents' massive silk-cotton tree when Grandpa Marcus hands me half a calabash, which was probably grown on my grandparents' land and has been plucked from one of their trees and has been hollowed out just for this moment.

Isabelle being here, in this way, momentarily feels like yet another return. It feels as though she had been sent on some kind of journey, as a rite of passage. Like she'd been told to go into a forest to retrace the footsteps of her ancestors and re-surface here, now, not as a young girl, but as a woman. Except she has not walked out of the forest on her own. We had to carry her here.

Mom tips a smaller version of the urn we left at home and sprinkles part of the ashes into the half calabash.

The last time Isabelle and I were both standing at this same spot, we'd introduced Grandpa Marcus and Grandma Régine to step dancing.

It was the end of the summer and we were about to leave. Everyone was sad. Isabelle thought that doing a little step dance for our grandparents would cheer them up.

We started slowly, rocking our bodies back and forth. Then we marched military style, loudly thumping our feet. We pounded our hands on our chests and legs as though our skins were drums. We kept moving faster, doing our best to echo each other's shoulder and hip gyrations. But as much as we tried, we didn't look like we were in sync or coordinated. As we yelled out suggestions for moves to each other, Grandma Régine said we were acting as though we were possessed.

Every time I think of something like this, I feel like Isabelle is with me. At least for a little while. Then I have to let her go.

Now, standing in my grandparents' garden, I'm being asked to let go of her again. And on our birthday, too. Our fingers are being pried apart, just as they were in the car that night, just as they'd been on the day we were born.

I tug at the two necklaces around my neck, then cup my palms around the half calabash while looking at the faces around me. Dad shifts his weight on the cane he now uses and nods his head, signaling that it's okay for me to let go. The smaller urn is locked in the crook of Mom's elbow, but Dad is holding her other hand. Their fingers are so intertwined that unless you're looking closely you might miss the glint of their wedding bands.

Dad leans over and kisses Mom's cheek. They look at each other, and their teary eyes and half smiles make me think that Aunt Leslie is right, that their MO will probably kick in. Maybe Dad will now spend more time at home, and with both me and Isabelle out of the house, Mom will figure out what she wants to do next.

I can't help but feel that it's Isabelle's MO that has brought them back together. Aunt Leslie and Dr. Aidoo, too. Dr. Aidoo, who, it turns out, is rather quiet when no one's half-unconscious in a hospital bed. Dr. Aidoo, whose presence on the trip everyone has quietly come to accept.

That particular development would have really stunned Isabelle. We've had so much pain, she might have said, that maybe everyone is looking for love, capital L-O-V-E. Aunt Leslie and Dr. Aidoo, Uncle Patrick, Alejandra, Grandma Régine, and Grandpa Marcus all bow their heads and keep their eyes on the grass, where parts of Isabelle will soon land. The parts of her that will not blow away. The parts of her that will grow roots and become flowers here, the parts of her that will forever rest in the shadow of the silk-cotton tree.

Although I wear them less and less now, I'm glad that I have my cat eyes on. I look up at the sky, and even through the dark lenses, I can see a cloudless periwinkle sky.

A warm breeze blows over us that, if I just keep standing there, might possibly sweep the ashes out of the calabash before I get a chance to scatter them myself.

I wish I could puff Isabelle away like a dandelion floret. I wish I could blow into her like a balloon. I wish I could watch her float away on her own, towards that periwinkle sky. I wish she'd jump out from behind one of those trees and tell me exactly how to do this.

I want to sprinkle a dusting of her over the passion vines. I want to dash some over the azaleas, and a little more over the yellow oleanders. But most of all, I want to just stand there with her still holding my hand. And even as I tilt the calabash and the midday breeze starts sweeping the ashes away, I want them to come back to us and dance around us like pixie dust.

I am doing this wrong of course, now scattering willy-nilly, in front of me, behind me, on either side of me, into and against the breeze. But Isabelle will eventually do what she wants to do anyway. She will land wherever she wants. Somewhere I can't guide her to.

Looking at the rest of my family members, both old and new, I can't help but smile while they each try to wipe away tiny particles of Isabelle now clinging to their faces, dots of sand-like grains that once might have been her skin, glints of beige that were once her bones.

The sun is beating down hard. We are all sweating like crazy, and the sweat and ash combination makes us look like we're fetus-in-fetu marked, or are wearing partial Isabelle masks.

I imagine Isabelle looking down at all of us and laughing. I imagine her admiring how hard we're trying to hold on to her, to let go of her only one speck, one particle at a time.

Somewhere out there, I know she must be whispering, "Stun me. Stun me."

We're certainly trying.

CHAPTER 35

BEFORE WE HAVE lunch, we all shower and change out of our now Isabelle-covered clothes. Grandma Régine assigns bedrooms and everyone pairs off effortlessly.

Mom and Dad will be in the bedroom Dad and Uncle Patrick once shared. Uncle Patrick opts for some other rarely used room, as does Aunt Leslie. I will sleep in the room I have always shared with Isabelle, the one where we slept in the same queen-size, four-poster bed with a mosquito net draped over the canopy, the room our grandparents told us was ours.

After every visit, Isabelle and I would purposely leave something behind to mark our territory, and when we'd return we would look for it in the place we had left it to see if it had been moved. Sometimes we'd leave clothes, books, CDs, handheld video games, things we thought we'd need to fill endless hours of boredom that never came, since Grandpa Marcus and Grandma Régine always had us programmed for drop-in visits with their friends or road trips.

It's kind of bizarre to see Dr. Aidoo walking around my grandparents' garden in his khaki shorts and plaid cotton shirt. He looks curiously at ease, hungrily taking everything in. He looks like someone who's coming home to a place he never knew was his. Maybe Aunt Leslie has described this place to him. I can almost hear her preparing him for what he would see.

We are going to stay, she might have told him, in this impossibly large house on top of a hill, in a place where few other people have houses like this, where there's a beautiful garden, almost like a secret garden, on top of a broken city, in this country that is still beautiful though it isn't supposed to be.

This, if he had been able to access her brain, is also how Isabelle might have described this place to Dr. Aidoo. This is how she may have described it to Ron Johnson or anyone else she cared about. And there was a lot of Aunt Leslie in Isabelle and a lot of Isabelle in Aunt Leslie.

As the only non-blood or marital relatives among us, Dr. Aidoo and Alejandra drift away from the rest of us for a minute, maybe to compare notes.

The family pairings break up and reassemble around me. They couple and uncouple as brothers and sisters, husbands and wives, boyfriends and girlfriends. I am the only uncoupled one, alone, though they try not to make me feel that way, unyoked, untwined, without my sister.

If Isabelle were here, I would be with her and when we'd approach one of these couplings, it wouldn't seem strange at all. I would not be the odd girl out. But I am. Even as we sit down for a late lunch around a long, benched table on my grandparents' terrace, a table that usually sits twelve.

Grandma Régine puts me at the head of the table with one of my parents on each side. My parents' bodies buffer me again, but not enough to make me forget that instead of Grandpa Marcus, it would be Isabelle sitting at the opposite end of the table, placed as far away from me as possible, so that she and I would have no choice but to speak to other people.

The others do their best to fill out the table, crowding the empty spaces so that it seems like no one is missing, that everyone who is supposed to be here already is.

Grandma Régine likes to say that empty spaces at tables where people are eating leave room for wandering spirits to join in, spirits who are hungry for more than food, spirits who are hungry for company.

As the food is served by my grandparents' two elderly cooks, Delira and Annaise, I notice Grandma Régine sliding away from Uncle Patrick and moving closer to Dad, leaving a body-size gap, a space wide enough for another person to sit down next to her.

At the lunch, which is supposed to be a combination birthday celebration and wake, some of us tell stories about Isabelle. We barter our grief, exchanging pieces of her that were solely ours.

"Remember when . . ." we say.

"Remember when the two of you had the Hula-Hoop competition on your thirteenth birthday?" Grandma Régine starts off in English so everyone can understand. "Your bones ached so much you both couldn't walk the next day."

"Remember when Isabelle took off her shoes and handed them to that woman in front of the cathedral in Cap Haitien," Grandpa Marcus says.

I remember Isabelle, Grandma Régine, Grandpa Marcus, and I stepping out of Cap Haïtien's main cathedral one afternoon. We were surrounded by a group of people begging for money and food. Isabelle saw a barefoot woman with a tiny baby in her arms, a baby so bald and skinny that it would have been impossible to tell whether it was a boy or a girl, if not for the piece of white string looped like a teardrop earring around a small hole in each of her ears. Isabelle looked down at the woman's mud-crusted feet, then at her own. Isabelle and the woman and I had what looked like the same size feet. Isabelle took off her leopard print ballet flats—no, my leopard print ballet flats, which she'd borrowed without my permission—and handed them to the woman. The woman was so shocked that she didn't accept the shoes until some people started urging her to, by shouting that they would take the shoes if she didn't.

Isabelle didn't like us to tell that story. It was a cheesy story, she said, one that made her seem like she was trying to be a saint, when she'd only acted on impulse.

The shoes weren't even hers. They were mine. No one but Isabelle and I remembered that part. Still, it hadn't occurred to me to give away the shoes I was wearing.

If she'd had money with her that day, Isabelle would have given it all to that woman. How come I didn't remember that when I was pouting in Dad's car that evening when we were on our way to our school's spring orchestra concert?

The cathedral and shoes story reminds Aunt Leslie of the failed monarch butterfly pilgrimage, then the trip to Guanajuato. Uncle Patrick remembers our blizzard day at his apartment in Brooklyn.

Mom and Dad remain quiet. Too much must be coming to mind, too fast. It must be hard to choose.

Then Dad remembers how when we were nine, Isabelle and I woke up one morning and thought we were shrinking. We both looked at our hands and feet and shrieked, terrified that we were aging backwards and would turn into babies again. This happened after one of Isabelle's nightmares had spilled not just into my head but also into daybreak.

Dad lined us up against the giraffe-shaped measurement chart on the inside of our bedroom door. He noticed that we'd actually grown, half an inch since the last time.

"Sometimes things happen backwards in dreams," Dad had told us. "Whenever I dream that I'm going to a funeral, I'm sure to have one of the best days of my life."

I wonder if his dreams still work that way.

Mom chimes in with a story about mirrors.

Mom used to tape mirror boards inside our cribs when we were babies. She remembers how when Izzie was with me, I'd tap my fingers against Izzie's forehead the same way I did the mirror's surface. Most babies think they're seeing someone else when they look into a mirror. Izzie and I must have thought we were holding our 3-D reflections whenever we touched each other.

We were junior scientists in elementary school, Dad tags on. We'd ask him and Mom for kits and books on how to split water, make crystals, turn water into fake wine.

We also made invisible ink with baking soda, Mom reminds him. We made lava lamps and volcanoes, hot-air balloons with tissue paper.

They're only telling stories about Isabelle and me together. (Do they know any stories that are only Giselle stories or only Isabelle stories?) They make us sound like magicians.

They make us sound magical, too.

"You guys used to sing a lot together, just the two of you," Mom says, keeping her eyes on me. "Do you remember?"

Of course I remember.

Our middle school music classes were once-a-week group guitar lessons. I gave up the guitar pretty quickly, assigning myself the role of Isabelle's occasional vocalist. I'd make up monosyllabic songs as Isabelle would clang away, playing the same three notes over and over again.

In the house!

Clang! Clang! Clang!

In the clouds!

Clang! Clang! Clang!

In the house that's in the clouds!

Clang! Clang! Clang! Clang! Clang! Clang! Clang!

When it seems like it might be my turn to speak, I try to stammer out a few words about how Isabelle and I would stand on my grandparents' porch, lather up our hair, strip down to our underwear, and then step out in the rain. Grandpa Marcus and Grandma Régine even joined us once, giggling nervously as they wondered how Mom and Dad would react if they saw the four of us out there, dancing in our undies in the rain.

"We knew you were doing that," Dad says, in part to spare me the tsunami of tears he sees coming my way.

"We know everything," Mom says, then chuckles.

I absolutely believe her.

Grandma Régine spares us all the agony of names and candles and the choice of having one or two birthday cakes. Instead, we are served pieces of her vanilla-coconut cake, Isabelle's favorite. Then everyone sings "Happy Birthday" to Isabelle, and after ninety seconds, timed by Grandma Régine, they sing "Happy Birthday" to me. Just as we'd always done in the past.

Next year they might have to sing for me first. I am now officially older than Isabelle.

That night I lie in bed with my parents, under their mosquito net. I look up, into the dark, and try to find traces of the white ceiling above us. If Isabelle were here, I'd be in bed with her, doing the same thing, as she slept. I'd also be looking for the stray fireflies, which sometimes got into the rooms and lit up small fragments of the walls.

My parents aren't asleep, but they don't move or speak, so I don't move or speak, either.

Sometime in the middle of the night, I hear a single mosquito buzzing in my left ear.

I imagine that Isabelle is this mosquito, which is brave enough to have sneaked under the net and trapped itself in with us. I know that from now on, I will always want to find some trace of Isabelle in everything that lives and breathes and tries to get close to me. I know I will listen for her breath in every piece of music. I will look for her face in flowers, inside every church, every cathedral, in the movements of every cat, butterfly, dolphin, or pilot whale. I will always look for signs that she's working full-time trying to pierce this impossible veil between her and me.

I love you, I will want to say, even to mosquitoes. Though it might be easier to say to fireflies.

I slide to the bottom of the bed, raise the net, and climb out. I feel my way through the pitch-black room towards the door.

My parents say nothing to each other or to me. I hear them fumbling behind me in the dark, following me towards the door and maybe towards those fireflies, which are possibly waiting for me on the silk-cotton tree. I think of my parents' bodies merging into a new version of Isabelle—Isabelle 2.0— an Isabelle that can appear and disappear, in whatever form she likes, at will.

I walk back to the bed and lie down.

My parents do, too.

CHAPTER 36

THE NEXT DAY the Marshalls arrive with Tina in tow. I can tell that this was planned a while back. My parents had already anticipated their need for reinforcements. They also know how hard it will be for me to make new friends from now on. They don't want me to lose two sisters at once.

Tina comes out and tells me all of this as we slip into each other's arms. For the first time since Isabelle died, I allow myself to really cry, my shoulders rising and falling with each new wave of tears.

I point to a shady corner of the garden, and Tina follows me there. I show her the spots on the grass where some of Isabelle landed, where the earth has already swallowed her up, and the morning dew has since washed her away.

"I know we have more." I say this about the ashes, but about our memories, too.

I find the concave ridge in the silk-cotton tree where Isabelle and I once carved our names. Huge, crooked capital letters stare back at us. Isabelle's hollowed-out name is on top of mine, with only a few inches between them. It had taken us days to carve our names with one of Grandpa Marcus's Swiss Army knives.

We considered carving a heart around our names, but Grandma Régine said that a heart might bind us even more and might lead to our spending the rest of our lives together, two old maids in a house full of cats.

Since Mom had taken Dessalines over to the Marshalls' before we left, I ask Tina what they've done with him.

Pastor Ben is watching him, she says, and he and Dessalines are going to get along just fine.

I was hoping she would tell me that Jean Michel was taking care of Dessalines so I could ask about him, too.

She senses this and tells me anyway.

"I'm so sorry about that whole thing," she says. "I should have spoken up in the museum that day. And even afterwards."

"I didn't give you a chance to," I say.

"He never liked me that way," she says. "He liked you. He still likes you. When you said what you said, we both felt like you just wanted us to go away. We did try to go away, but separately, not together. Remotely."

We find a cool spot under the tree, where the midday heat has not yet penetrated the ground. I try to show her how we can both hug the tree trunk and still not touch hands in the middle. She takes off her ladybug-shaped fanny pack and drops it on the ground so her entire body can touch the tree.

In the museum that day, I had been just as unrecognizable to her as I had been to myself.

"He likes you, not me," she says again.

Sisters before dudes, after all.

She picks up her fanny pack from the ground.

"I called him to let him know I was coming here," she says. "And he sent you something."

I want to tell her how cute her ladybug fanny pack is, but I'm too excited to see what he's sent me. My heart is beating too fast.

"Calm down," she says. "It's not a bar of gold."

"And probably not a bar of soap." I try to make a joke. "Nor a bar of candy, a candy bar."

I realize how much I will miss her during the next school year, how much I will miss him, too. We won't be making any college plans together and we won't be going to our prom together, just as I will not be doing any of those things with Isabelle.

Tina hands me a framed picture, half the size of a postcard. In the red plastic frame is a shrunken copy of Frida Kahlo's *The Two Fridas*.

The Fridas' hearts, more than their faces, pop out at me, one heart crimson and pumping bright red blood and the other darkened, lifeless, and nearly drained.

I wonder which Frida he is.

I wonder which Frida I am.

"I almost didn't bring it," Tina says. "I know that's his screen saver, but he didn't send a note with it or anything. He just said you'd figure it out."

It takes me a while to figure it out, but eventually I do. I think he's trying to tell me what everyone's been telling me in one way or another since Isabelle died, that I won't be the bloodless Frida forever, that one day, my heart will be full of life again. He could also be telling me that Isabelle might have survived the crash, only to endure a life full of devastation and pain, something that still remains a possibility for the rest of us.

I run these theories by Tina, who says, "Why couldn't he just text or email you? Or even write something down on a piece of paper? Or on the back of this thing? Not everything needs to remain unsaid."

"He likes being cryptic." I find myself defending him. "Maybe that's why it was so easy for him to help us find Janice."

Other people's mysteries are sometimes easier to solve than our own.

Tina and I sit there, in that cool spot under the silk-cotton tree, for what feels like hours. I tell her everything that's happened since I tried to ban her from my heart. I tell her about the organ donation letter, the flute case, the state attorney's decision, all of which she already knows from her parents, who've been told everything by my parents.

We survey the horizon and look down at different parts of the city, the stacked houses below, the mountains, then the sea.

Soon, it starts raining over the sea, just as Isabelle and I had seen it rain many times before.

Tina and I walk to the edge of the property, as far as a steep cliff above a low concrete wall. We look out over the sea as a widening circle forms around the shrouded sun, in a hazy combination of lilac, emerald, scarlet, and gold.

"Is that some kind of rainbow?" Tina asks.

"It's called a glory," I say.

"That's beyond cool," she says.

"Isabelle and I have seen a lot of them."

I remember Grandpa Marcus telling Isabelle and me how we're able to see so many glories because of the height and angle of the property. Because he believed that architecture should be part of the physical poetry of everyday life, he'd picked the land and designed the house with natural wonders in mind, including rainbows and glories.

The first time Tina, Isabelle, and I all saw somebody die, we were seven years old. Our families were at the beach together near Aunt Leslie's house in Orlando. A little girl, who looked like she was a year or two younger than us, had spent the entire morning digging a body-size hole for herself in the sand near the beach chairs where her mother and father were reading and sunbathing. The girl and her parents would take breaks, run to the water and swim for a while, but the little girl would come back and start digging again until she could sit in the hole without us seeing her head from a few feet away.

We weren't looking when it happened, but at some point her sand hole collapsed. The hole quickly filled in around her and the little girl disappeared.

Mom, Dad, Aunt Leslie, the Marshalls, and a bunch of other people immediately joined the little girl's parents and started digging for her with their bare hands. The sand must have shifted because the little girl was no longer where she was supposed to be.

Right before Fire Rescue arrived, Dad and Mr. Marshall found the little girl. When they pulled her out, she looked like a sand mummy doll. Aunt Leslie tried her best to resuscitate her, but it was too late.

I think this is why Mom and Dad didn't want Isabelle to be buried. They didn't want her beneath the ground where nature's wrath might further attack her body and where things like this glory might be kept from her view.

I imagine Isabelle seeing more glories now, and many more things that the rest of us still have no idea how to name. I imagine her making beautiful things, too, out of whatever brush or brew that you're given to paint the sky with when you die.

Tina and I stare at the glory until the rain stops falling into the sea and the sun starts crawling out from behind the clouds. The glory begins to fade and all the colors blur into a dull grey. Like when you're twirling a rainbow-colored spinning top and all the shades merge into one, because the colors are moving too quickly for your eyes to keep up.

My whole world has been like that for a while. Spinning too fast for both my brain and my heart to keep up. I close my eyes and try to make the glory last, knowing that when I open them again, it will be gone.

"Close your eyes, too," I tell Tina.

"What?"

"Just do it," I say and she does.

"Are you going to push me down this mountain?" she asks anyway.

"It's not a mountain," I say. "And I'm not going to push you off of it. Just keep your eyes closed."

"What are we doing?" she asks.

"We're each going to say half a goodbye to the glory."

"I didn't realize we'd said hello to it," she says.

"Just do it," I say.

"How's that?"

"It's for Isabelle," I say, knowing that she'd start making fun of me otherwise.

I tell her about Isabelle always not wanting to say a full good-bye to the glory, so that it would keep coming back.

"Okay, then," Tina says, still not sounding fully convinced.

"You will say 'Good,'" I say. "And I will say 'Bye.' And each of us will have said only half a goodbye, and not a full one."

When she finally gets the hang of it, I let her go first.

I keep my eyes closed and try to keep the glory fully and colorfully alive in my memory.

"Good?" Tina whispers.

"Bye," I say.

UNTWINE

EDWIDGE DANTICAT

A GUIDE FOR READERS AND BOOK CLUB GROUPS

QUESTIONS AND TOPICS
FOR DISCUSSION

1. How does the folktale of the firebird mirror the arc of Giselle's story?

2. Giselle sometimes seems to blame herself for the car accident; sometimes she almost blames her parents. Gloria/Janice was attempting to escape a horrible fate. Is there any one ultimate culprit?

3. When a relationship as long-lived and complex as Giselle's parents' begins to unravel, should they try to make it work? How do the accident and consequent events change the dynamics of their relationship?

4. Giselle's Haitian heritage plays a significant role in the book. How does this aspect of her identity influence other realms of her life—friendship, family, community, loss? What elements of identity make Giselle who she is? Who you are?

5. Giselle's art teacher mentions the stages of grief identified by psychologist Elizabeth Kübler-Ross: Denial and Isolation, Anger, Bargaining, Depression, and Acceptance. Do Giselle's stages of grief sync with that model? Do you believe these steps encompass the full breadth of grieving?

6. How does Isabelle's relationship with Ron change her relationship with Giselle?

7. Giselle cites her art teacher, Ms. Walker, who would say that to be good at drawing you need to simplify. How does Danticat use closely observed small details to create a larger portrait? Were there small observations about the sisters' lives that took on a larger meaning as the story progressed?

8. Why does Giselle think Jean Michel and Tina have fallen for each other? How have Jean Michel's feelings actually changed after the accident?

9. For a while, it seems like Gloria may have intentionally tried to kill the Boyers. If this had turned out to be true, would Giselle have ended up in the same place emotionally, or would the book have had a different ending?

10. Giselle says, "I've been saying goodbye to all of that since the crash. I've been saying goodbye all along." How were Giselle and Isabelle already beginning to "untwine" before the accident? Can the book be read as a metaphor for the way that all young adults preparing to head out into the world must detach themselves from their old lives? When have you had to "untwine" from someone?

A CONVERSATION WITH
EDWIDGE DANTICAT

SCHOLASTIC: Nationality and heritage seem to deeply influence your work. How did your Haitian nationality and cultural heritage influence the writing of *Untwine*, specifically the development of the characters, their relationships, and the story arc?

ED: When I was a teenager, I used to read both to find myself and to escape. But there was always something very special about discovering characters who were like me. I always found that jolt of recognition so validating and exciting. I often feel like I am writing for the teenage girl I once was, the one who was looking for herself in all kinds of books. That's why I tend to write about people who share my culture and heritage, characters who are like myself and my family and friends, people who are in my life every day but who I don't see enough in literature. I am also very proud of my culture and heritage, and I love to share elements of it. The Nobel laureate Toni Morrison has said that if there is a book you want to read, you should write it, so every book I write is a book that both the adult and teenage girl in me are dying to read.

SCHOLASTIC: As Giselle moves in and out of consciousness in the hospital, the narrative also moves in and out of time. How did you come to this particular structure for *Untwine*?

ED: I wanted to show Giselle as both still being part of her family and not being part of it. She is really floating in-between two states of existing. My mother was very sick while I was writing *Untwine*. She eventually died before the book was published. I saw her experience that state a bit, where you kind of want to hold on and also want to let go. My mother would drift in and out in the same way that Giselle does, and I could see her contemplating both the past and a possible future in which she wasn't sure she would exist. I came up with the structure while watching my mother go through the same thing.

SCHOLASTIC: The relationships between Giselle and Isabelle and their parents take on varied forms and dynamics throughout the course of the novel. Can you speak to this a bit?

ED: Every relationship is complicated. It would be nice if people simply loved each other and it was always okeydokey, but there are tensions and silences in every relationship. I don't have a sister. I have three younger brothers, but I have always wanted a sister. I've watched my friends with their sisters, and it's always fascinated me how they can be very close but also fight passionately then make up just as quickly. There are many twins in my world, and I've seen kind of the same thing, though some of the twins I know seem to have their own language and gestures for communicating, even while fighting. I think one is always forced to revisit and examine relationships more closely when a loved one is in danger, and that definitely happens to the sisters over time. And of course their relationship changes because they are also growing up and are interested in boys, which takes them out of their bubbles a bit.

SCHOLASTIC: Do you think Giselle and Isabelle's birth order impacts their relationship?

ED: I do. I think whatever the sibling relationship, if you're told you were first, you tend to try to live that role. I am the oldest of my siblings, and a lot of my sibling dynamics are based on the fact that I am expected to be a certain way because of our birth order. I think even though the girls were only born a very short time apart, they still assume the roles of older twin and younger twin.

SCHOLASTIC: How do you feel, from personal experience as well as writing this book and being inside Giselle's head, about the accuracy or truth of Elizabeth Kübler-Ross's description of the stages of grief: Denial and Isolation, Anger, Bargaining, Depression, and Acceptance?

ED: I think it's a bit too neat, which is why Giselle kind of rejects having it forced on her in the book. My father died eleven years ago, and sometimes I still want to pick up the phone and call him. Though I have accepted his death, I still feel like I am in denial at times. So while one might experience all of these things (or not), they may not come in that particular order. I think Kübler-Ross also missed terror or fear, which C. S. Lewis and others have talked about as a part of grieving. One of the things I felt most strongly while grieving my mother was a kind of fear that I too would end up dying soon after.

SCHOLASTIC: Do you consider your work more character or plot driven? When you sit down to write, do you tend to start with a character or an event?

ED: I think my books are plot driven, but then people keep telling me they are character driven. I like plot and story very much, and I think they're necessary and important, but I am also very interested in what my characters are feeling and thinking, and I do tend to linger on that. I am extremely interested in their interior lives. My books, though, tend to grow from the vision in my mind of one big scene that then drives the rest of the story toward its middle and conclusion.

SCHOLASTIC: How do you balance being a parent yourself with your career—writing, speaking, touring?

ED: I try out a lot of my stories first on my children, even the plots for my adult books. Sometimes they give me suggestions and other ideas. I do it with them in the car and at bedtime. I guess you might call that multitasking. I tell them they're my consultants. I also try to write a lot in my head while traveling or while at home doing something like cooking. So when I sit down to write, I'm halfway there and spend less time figuring things out.

SCHOLASTIC: What are the subjects you find yourself most concerned with or intrigued by in your work? Family? Fate? Death and life? Why do you think that is?

ED: All of the above. I am really interested in how families grow as a unit and how family members grow within that unit, especially when faced with separation, both with immigration and also tragedy. As an immigrant kid who has grown into an immigrant parent, it's interesting to me to see how families adapt and how they cohere or come apart across generations in this world that is home to the kids, but still somewhat new to their parents and grandparents. But I think life and death are my ultimate subjects. Though we are not always solely focused on them at all times, they are indeed the biggest pillars of our existence.

ACKNOWLEDGMENTS

Thanks to Lisa Sandell for writing me out of the blue one day to see if I might have a book like this in me. I am also deeply grateful to the beloved twins in my life: Alexis and Zoë Danticat, and Natalie and Adele Austin, for allowing me to directly and indirectly observe twin life. May they never have to go through anything remotely like the things that happen in this book.

I am grateful to Aimee Ferrer, Maggie Austin, and Kathy Strobach for all their help with legal information. Thank you, Patricia Engel, for some crucial advice. Thank you Fedo, Mira, Leila, and Madame Boyer for every second of every day. And thank you Manman, my Isabelle, for showing me what love, hope, and courage look like until the very end.